M000081448

HARRY HUNTER MYSTERY - BOOK 2

RUN GIRL RUN

WILLOW ROSE

Published by BUOY MEDIA LLC

Cover design by Juan Villar Padron,
https://www.juanjpadron.com

Special thanks to my editor Janell Parque
http://janellparque.blogspot.com/

Tired of too many emails? Text the word: "willowrose" to 31996 to sign up to Willow's VIP Text List to get a text alert with news about New Releases, Giveaways, Bargains and Free books from Willow.

Books by the Author

HARRY HUNTER MYSTERY SERIES

- All The Good Girls
- Run Girl Run
- No Other Way
- Never Walk Alone

MARY MILLS MYSTERY SERIES

- What Hurts the Most
- You Can Run
- You Can't Hide
- Careful Little Eyes

EVA RAE THOMAS MYSTERY SERIES

- Don't Lie to me
- What you did
- Never Ever
- Say You Love me
- Let Me Go
- It's Not Over
- Not Dead yet

EMMA FROST SERIES

- Itsy Bitsy Spider
- Miss Dolly had a Dolly
- Run, Run as Fast as You Can
- Cross Your Heart and Hope to Die
- Peek-a-Boo I See You
- Tweedledum and Tweedledee
- Easy as One, Two, Three
- There's No Place like Home
- Slenderman
- Where the Wild Roses Grow
- Waltzing Mathilda
- Drip Drop Dead
- Black Frost

JACK RYDER SERIES

- Hit the Road Jack
- Slip out the Back Jack
- The House that Jack Built
- Black Jack
- Girl Next Door
- Her Final Word
- Don't Tell

REBEKKA FRANCK SERIES

- One, Two...He is Coming for You
- Three, Four...Better Lock Your Door
- Five, Six...Grab your Crucifix
- Seven, Eight...Gonna Stay up Late
- Nine, Ten...Never Sleep Again
- Eleven, Twelve...Dig and Delve
- Thirteen, Fourteen...Little Boy Unseen
- Better Not Cry
- Ten Little Girls
- It Ends Here

MYSTERY/THRILLER/HORROR NOVELS

- Sorry Can't Save You
- In One Fell Swoop
- Umbrella Man
- Blackbird Fly
- To Hell in a Handbasket
- Edwina

HORROR SHORT-STORIES

- Mommy Dearest
- The Bird
- Better watch out
- Eenie, Meenie
- Rock-a-Bye Baby

- Nibble, Nibble, Crunch
- Humpty Dumpty
- Chain Letter

PARANORMAL SUSPENSE/ROMANCE NOVELS

- In Cold Blood
- The Surge
- Girl Divided

THE VAMPIRES OF SHADOW HILLS SERIES

- Flesh and Blood
- Blood and Fire
- Fire and Beauty
- Beauty and Beasts
- Beasts and Magic
- Magic and Witchcraft
- Witchcraft and War
- War and Order
- Order and Chaos
- Chaos and Courage

THE AFTERLIFE SERIES

- Beyond
- Serenity
- Endurance

- Courageous

THE WOLFBOY CHRONICLES

- A Gypsy Song
- I am WOLF

DAUGHTERS OF THE JAGUAR

- Savage
- Broken

Chapter 1

AT LEAST THEY weren't literally living *on* the street. At least they had a roof over their heads and a place to sleep. Even though it was tight inside the car, Emilia García didn't think it was as bad as when they had stayed in that apartment with three other families, sharing one bedroom, one bath, and one small kitchen.

"I'll pick you up at two-thirty, as usual. If I'm not here, then just wait a few minutes, okay?"

"Okay."

Emilia looked out the window of the station wagon as her mother drove up in front of the school. This was the tough part—getting dropped off. The other kids, on their way into school, always stopped and stared at the towels in the windows and the old rusty car. She feared that they could see all their belongings stashed in there when Emilia opened the door.

It was the fourteenth school Emilia had attended in just her eleven years on this earth.

"Have a great day, honey," her mother said as she stepped out of the car, keeping her head down and avoiding any eye contact at all cost.

Emilia sent her a smile, hoping to brighten up her mother's day. They had been living in their car for three months now, while her mother looked for a new job. Emilia's mom and dad had split up two years ago, and after a while, her mother hadn't been able to keep up with the bills. After that, they were constantly on the move. They were sleeping on friends' couches or in shelter after shelter. In one of the places where they stayed, a roommate tried to kill a neighbor while they were there, so finally, they had found out they liked sleeping in their car better than any of those places.

"You too, Mom. I love you."

"Love you too, baby."

Emilia slammed the door shut, then watched as the old station wagon drove away, making all kinds of odd noises as it went. A couple of girls from Emilia's class giggled as they passed her, and she looked away. She let them walk inside first before she followed them. Most people might think that school would be terrible for Emilia, since she didn't have any friends, and no one ever talked to her. But the fact was, Emilia loved school. She loved walking into the airconditioned building and feeling like a normal kid for a few hours. After a night in the warm car, she was usually sticky and sweaty and sick of the muggy Miami air. Inside the school building, no one knew she had been up at five o'clock, so they could go to a McDonalds to use the restroom and wash themselves. They didn't know she had been awake every hour during the night to make sure they were both safe, that no one was trying to steal what little they had or attack them. They didn't know that Emilia laid awake at night, listening to her mother's crying in the darkness.

"Welcome to class, students; please find your seats," the teacher said to the class while smiling at Emilia, who was her favorite student.

Emilia smiled back, feeling that strange soothing sensation like she was finally at home.

Here, she was just like everyone else. She was a student who had come to learn. And usually, she was able to forget—at least for a little while—how terrified she was of summer break, of her mother getting hurt when she wasn't there to protect her, or of not surviving another night. Here, she was able to forget all those things for a little while.

Though, there was one thing that she couldn't escape no matter where she went, no matter how much she tried.

The terrible thought of *that* guy finding them, the one with the steel-grey eyes and the big rough hands who kept reaching out for her in her nightmares.

Chapter 2

"EAT UP. YOU NEED IT, BABY."

Emilia looked down into the can of beans. She had only eaten half of its contents and could barely get herself to eat more. The smell alone made her want to throw up. Cold beans eaten directly from the can was her least favorite meal. Not that she could afford to be picky; she should be happy that she even got any food.

Emilia forced a smile and looked at her mom across the cabin of the old station wagon. They had turned the back into a living area by putting the seats down and hanging towels in front of the windows, so no one could look in. It was so hot in there all afternoon, and they couldn't wait till the sun went down. Emilia and her mom had spent the afternoon walking the streets and going into stores to cool down. That way, they didn't have to get in the car till just before sundown.

The AC only worked when the engine was turned on, and they couldn't afford the gas to drive around except when going somewhere important like to school or looking for jobs for her mom.

Emilia took one more bite, then swallowed, closing her eyes, barely chewing, so she tasted it as little as possible.

"I'm not hungry anymore," she said and handed her mother the can. Her mother gave her a look.

"Are you sure? It's all we have."

She nodded, even though she felt her stomach rumbling. The school served breakfast, and she still had half a muffin in her backpack she could eat at night if she woke up starving as she usually did. Emilia felt bad for not telling her mom about the muffin, but she needed it to make it through the night.

"Yes."

"Suit yourself."

Her mother ate the rest of her beans, shoveling the last part into her mouth, tipping the can upside down. Some of the red sauce ran down her chin, and she wiped it with her finger, then licked it.

Emilia winced when seeing this. Everything about them and the way they lived was so embarrassing.

Emilia leaned back and closed her eyes in shame, hoping the temperature would go down soon. They had popped both windows open in the front to let in some air. But no wind moved outside, so it didn't help much. Emilia was sweating heavily and felt tired. She peeked out from behind one of the towels and looked into the parking lot where they had decided to stay for the night. They usually shifted around, so the police wouldn't realize they were living there and chase them away. Tonight, they had chosen to park at the port. Emilia never liked sleeping there much. She preferred the parking lot at Walmart, where she felt safer. Down here, it was so vacant. They were surrounded by huge containers and enormous ships, but it all seemed so big and scary. Emilia thought about her day at school and was looking forward to going back the next day. But with every day that passed, they came closer to the weekend, and Emilia hated the weekends. The days drifting around with nothing to do were long and painful.

"Do you have homework?" her mother asked.

"Already did it at school," Emilia said. She failed to mention she had to do it at school since it was required to be done on a computer. She didn't want her mother to feel like a failure more than she already did.

"Maybe we should just call it a night, huh?" her mother said. "Get some sleep? It seems to be cooling down a little now already. There's a breeze coming from the water. I think it'll be real nice in a minute or two. I'll leave the windows cracked open for the night."

Emilia nodded. There was no point in staying awake because they had nothing to do. Emilia was exhausted anyway from waking up so many times the night before when her mother was crying. She really hoped she could just doze off now and not wake up till it was light out again, and the day had begun. She needed to drift off into the world of her dreams, where she'd forget about how miserable her life was.

They used a toilet on the port to brush their teeth and go to the bathroom before bedtime, then got back inside the car and locked the doors.

Her mother leaned over and kissed her in the darkness before she grabbed her pill bottle and took a couple. They were sleeping pills, which her mother often took before bedtime because she needed to sleep heavily. She couldn't afford to take them often, so it only happened on some days.

"Good night, sweetie. See you tomorrow."

"Good night, Mommy," Emilia sighed while secretly praying for sleep to come quickly. "I love you."

"Love you too."

Chapter 3

EMILIA WAS SLEEPING SOUNDLY when it happened. She was dreaming about her father, about the time before he and her mom split up, and those were the best dreams she could have. He was holding her in his arms, swinging her around like he always used to do when she was younger. And he was laughing. Emilia barely remembered him laughing anymore since, in the end, before her parents split up, no one ever laughed in her house anymore. And her mother had barely laughed since.

They were in the middle of a deep hug, her father and her, when she felt movement. In her dream, it resulted in an earthquake, and she felt herself getting stirred up with fear. Her dad didn't seem to feel it. He just kept hugging her and laughing, and she had to yell at him to let him know there was an earthquake. Still, he didn't let her go, and she felt so safe in his arms, even though the entire earth shook beneath them.

"Dad?" she said in the dream. "I think something is wrong."

"No, sweetie; we're fine. We're safe here," he said, smiling. The sight of his smile calmed her. But then another thought struck her, one she couldn't escape.

Mom? Where is Mom?

Her heart began to race in her chest as she realized her mother was nowhere to be seen.

"Mom?" she called out as the earth shook even stronger beneath her. "Mom?"

Now it felt like it wasn't just the ground beneath them that shook; it was the entire universe.

"What's happening? Dad? What's going on?"

As she turned to look in her dream, she spotted her dad suddenly far away as the ground opened up and swallowed him. She watched him disappear, screaming, then woke up inside the car, heart pounding in her chest, gasping for air.

"Dad? Mom? Mom?"

She opened her eyes just in time to feel the push. She gasped and pulled the towel aside, only to see the edge of the dock disappear behind them and someone standing on that dock looking down at her. A face she knew a little too well.

A face with deep-set steel-grey eyes.

Emilia gasped fearfully and then heard the loud

sound of the car plunging into the water. Paralyzed with panic, Emilia stared into the darkness as the car sunk. It took a few seconds for her to figure out what was going on, that this was no longer a dream.

Then, she screamed.

"M-O-O-O-M!"

She reached over and shook her mother, but she wouldn't wake up. The sleeping pills had knocked her out completely, and when that happened, Emilia knew there was no way she could wake her.

"Mom, please," she moaned as the car sunk deeper and deeper into the water, and some of it started to spurt in through the cracks. It was creaking and making all kinds of scary noises outside the car while Emilia panicked inside.

"Please, Mommy; please, wake up! I think we're drowning, Mommy. I think we're...please, wake up."

But her mother didn't wake up. Emilia whimpered and held her tightly as the water slowly filled the cabin of the car. She cried and tried to open the door, but it wouldn't budge. Emilia kicked and screamed as her clothes were soaked, and soon, she could barely keep her head above water.

THREE WEEKS LATER

Chapter 4

"GIRL FOURTEEN, ACUTE CARDIAC ARREST."

I was running behind the stretcher as I heard the paramedic give the message to the nurse in the ER. I don't know if it was hearing him say the words that made me finally break down and cry, or if it was the sight of them rushing my daughter down the hallway, asking me to stay back, that did it to me.

I leaned forward, hands resting on my knees, still panting, when Jean came out to the waiting room and saw me. We hadn't seen each other for weeks, and as her eyes fell on me, I started crying even harder.

"Harry!"

She rushed to me, grabbed me in her arms, and helped me sit down. It wasn't an easy thing to do with a big guy who's six-foot-eight and weighs more than two hundred and thirty pounds. Especially not for a small woman like Jean. But Jean was a lot stronger than you'd think. She spoke with a shivering voice.

"What happened? I saw them rush someone down to surgery. It looked like… Was that Josie?"

I nodded, gasping for air. I could hardly get the words across my lips and struggled to tell her.

"Sh-she fell. They have an important volleyball game next week. She had just been out running, then came back into the yard where I was sitting, then she just fell. It was like she deflated. I…I don't understand. I…I…she wasn't breathing; she was completely gone. There was no pulse or anything, Jean; she was just lifeless. I frantically performed CPR. I was so scared; you have no idea. But I got her heart beating again while my dad called for help. The paramedics came and rushed her into the ambulance…her heart kept shutting down, they said, and they barely managed to keep her alive." I looked into Jean's eyes. They were filled with worry and fear. She was breathing heavily. Jean cared for my daughter almost as much as I did. I continued, my voice cracking:

"What's happening to her? She was fine this morning, and then she said she'd…go for a run…and now this? What's happening to my baby?"

Jean grabbed my hands in hers, and I leaned my head on her shoulder. I could tell she was moved too. Jean was a nurse at the ER, but she was also my neighbor, and we had been very close until recently. Until my wife, Camille, woke up from her brain-injury coma due to an overdose three years ago, Jean had been the one taking care of us all. But now that my wife was better and was awake, Jean had pulled away. Maybe because we had kissed, maybe because we had decided to start dating the moment before Camille awoke.

Sitting here, I suddenly missed Jean more than ever.

"What's happening to her?" I asked. "Will she be all right?"

Jean took a deep breath. It was obvious that she was shaken. "She's in good hands. That much, I know. They took her into surgery right away."

"Tell me she's going to be all right, Jean. I won't be able to live without her. She's my everything."

"I know, hon," she said. "I know. They're doing all they can."

The doors to the ER slid open, and my dad stepped inside, looking distressed. My dad, the retired pastor, who was always there for me…who was always there with an encouraging word or ready to step in when I needed someone to look after Camille or my daughter, Josie. He was, in many ways, the rock I leaned on, and I wouldn't know how to do all this without him by my side.

"I drove here as fast as I could," he said and hugged Jean when he saw her. "Any news?"

"Not yet," Jean said. "I'll go check now and keep you posted, okay?"

"Thank you; you're an angel," my dad said, holding Jean's hands in his. He had always been very fond of Jean, so much so that he was the one who pushed for me to start dating her, even though Camille was lying upstairs in a vegetative state.

"I told Camille," he said when Jean was gone. "Before I left."

"And?"

"She seemed upset, but I'm not sure she fully understood."

I nodded. Camille was awake, yes, and had been for about a month. It was an answer to our prayers, a miracle even, but she hadn't been the same since she woke up. She was still unable to control her body and could only be pushed around in a wheelchair. She could barely speak and mostly just said our daughter's name; that was all, and she struggled to understand what was going on around her and things we told her. The doctor told us it would require lots of rehabilitation, and that we shouldn't expect her ever to be completely herself again. He also said that her reaction would be different to things, and we couldn't always count on it. She could be smiling yet be sad without us knowing it because she couldn't control her reactions the way other people could.

"She might have understood it," I said. "But she just couldn't react the way you thought she would."

My dad sighed and put his hand on my shoulder. "I'm sure you're right, son. I'm sure you're right."

I knew how he felt about Camille. He still believed I should put her in a nursing home, where they'd know how to take proper care of her. I think he still had a hard time forgiving her for doing drugs again, when she had been clean for years, and thereby ruining my life and Josie's. I was struggling with that part as well if I was completely honest. Even though I didn't like to admit it since she was the one with the brain injury, she was the one trapped inside of her body. I had hoped to get some answers out of her when she finally woke up, but so far, I knew nothing about what happened or why she had started to do drugs again when we were doing so well together. Our life had been perfect up until that point.

Why would she risk destroying our family?

"Here's the doctor," my dad said as the door opened, and someone came inside wearing a doctor's coat. We were the only ones in the waiting room, and the man in the white coat turned to look at us, then approached us with worried eyes.

The way he looked at me made my stomach churn. It didn't seem like it was going to be good news.

Chapter 5

"MR. HUNTER?"

"That's me. How's she doing, Doctor?"

"Not good, I'm afraid," he said. His nametag said, Dr. Scott. He was about half my size and had lips that turned down at the corners, giving the impression of a permanent pout. "She suffered sudden cardiac arrest a second time after she was brought in. We were able to get her stabilized. I'm afraid she has ARVC, a type of inherited Cardiomyopathy. It can cause sudden heart failure, especially in teens and young adults. We were lucky that she was brought in so quickly. In many of these cases, which often occur in young athletes, they don't make it to the hospital alive."

I barely breathed or blinked.

"Heart failure…but…her heart has always been

fine. She's been running and playing volleyball for years?"

Doctor Scott sighed and smiled politely. "Unfortunately, it's the same story that we often hear in these types of cases. Does your family have a history of heart disease?"

"Not mine, but I don't know about my wife's. She has no contact with her family, so we have no way of knowing."

"You might want to ask her or have her heart checked as well."

I stared at him, not knowing what to tell him. I couldn't possibly ask Camille about her family history of illness. I mean, I could, but she wouldn't be able to answer. I felt so lost.

"But what does this mean?" my dad asked. "Is Josie going to be well?"

Doctor Scott sighed again. "Not unless she gets a new heart. I'm putting her name on the transplant list, and due to the urgency, she'll get to the top of the list, but unfortunately, it can take months to find one. I'm not sure she has that long. I'm sorry. I wish I had better news."

"Is there nothing else you can do, Doctor?" my dad asked.

"Normally, I'd say we could try the implantation of a ventricular assist device, a mechanical pump attached directly to the heart. Though the device can provide improved circulation support until a donor heart is found, the surgery would be particularly risky, due to the condition of Josie's heart. I wouldn't recommend it."

"Doctor Scott," a nurse called when coming through the doors.

"Listen, we'll do everything in our power to find your daughter a new heart," Doctor Scott said, ending the conversation, "but right now, I'm needed elsewhere. You can see her as soon as she wakes up in the ICU, which shouldn't be too long. The nurses will take you to her."

"Thank you, Doctor; thank you for all you've done." I shook the doctor's hand, and he left. I stared after him, my heart sinking. My daughter had heart failure? How did I not know this till now?

God, please. Find a heart for Josie. Save her!

I sat down, feeling heavy, hiding my face between my hands, praying under my breath for a miracle when Jean came out to us.

"She needs a new heart," my dad said. "You just missed the doctor."

"I know," Jean said. "I heard."

She sat down next to me and placed a warm hand on my shoulder. "I am so sorry, Harry."

"He said it could take months to find one, even though she's so sick that they'll put her at the top of the list. Is that really true?" my dad asked.

She nodded with a deep exhale. "I'm afraid so."

I shook my head. "I can't believe it. She survived, and now she might die…because they can't find a heart?"

"Many patients die while on the transplant list, I'm afraid." Jean swallowed. She looked around her briefly, then said. "Listen, we might have one here locally at the hospital."

I raised my eyebrows as I lifted my head and looked at her.

"What do you mean?"

She grabbed my hand in hers. "Come with me. I'll show you."

Chapter 6

JEAN TOOK us down the hallway to the ICU, then opened the door to one of the rooms. Inside lay a girl, a couple of years younger than Josie, on full life-support. Her eyes were closed, her breathing orchestrated solely by machines.

"She's been here for three weeks," she said. "She's been declared clinically brain dead by our doctors. She'll never wake up, they say. There's no brain activity, and she can't even breathe on her own, but her heart is working fine."

I stared at the young girl, feeling awful. I felt terrible for her; she was nothing but a child. Her parents had to be devastated.

"What happened to her?"

"She drowned," Jean said. "I don't know all the details, but I do know that they pulled her and her mother out of the harbor three weeks ago. I heard they were in their car. The mother was dead when they pulled them out, but the girl's heart was still beating, so they brought her in. They don't know what to do with her since no relatives have claimed her. They can't shut her off till someone gives their consent."

"So, what are you thinking?" I asked. It was strange to look at this girl when my own was fighting for her life as well here in the same hospital.

Jean gave me a look. "Well, she has a perfectly functioning heart, and Josie needs one, right? She's the right blood type too. I checked."

"Is she a donor?"

"Not yet."

"But you just said that she has no relatives, and they can't do anything without their consent," my dad said.

Jean smiled and tilted her head.

"She wants me to find them," I said, "then persuade them to donate her heart, and hopefully, it'll be given to Josie, who is at the top of the transplant list."

"You're the detective, aren't you?" Jean said. "I bet if anyone can find them, it's definitely you."

I exhaled and nodded. It was tough to have to make a decision like this, especially for me, a pastor's son who believed in miracles and the power of prayer. But I also believed in my daughter's survival and would do anything to make sure she didn't die. It was an ethical dilemma that I couldn't afford to have.

"I say it's worth a try, at least," Jean said. "They can always say no."

"I don't know about this," my dad said skeptically. "Haven't the police looked for them already?"

"Probably," Jean said. "But so far, they haven't found them, and I have a feeling Harry can. It's a long shot, but better than nothing, the way I see it."

"A long shot is better than no shot at all; that's for sure. Do you have a name?" I asked. "The name of the girl?"

"Emilia García."

"And the mother?" I asked. "The one that died?"

Jean shook her head. "I'm afraid I don't know."

I nodded pensively.

"I'll find it and the relatives, if it's the last thing I do."

Chapter 7

I OPENED the door without knocking. My boss, Major Fowler, lifted his eyes and looked at me as I burst into his office, located on the third floor of the building housing the Miami Police Department on 2nd Avenue. It was Sunday, but I knew he always came in for a few hours to get ready for the coming week. He liked the quietness of the office on Sundays, he had told me.

"Hunter? What are you doing here? Isn't this your day off?"

I stepped toward his desk. "It is. But something's come up. I need your help."

Fowler leaned back in his chair. We had known each other forever, and even though he had gone from dark brown to salt and pepper over the years, the way he lifted his eyebrows when looking at me was still the same.

"What's going on?"

"I don't have time to explain everything, but to make it quick, Josie was put in the hospital today. It's her heart."

Fowler went pale. "Oh, dear God. I am so sorry, Hunter. Let me know if I can do anything for you."

I rubbed my face, feeling sweaty from rushing to the police department downtown on my motorcycle. It was February, but Miami didn't care. The air outside was heavy, and the sun scorched from the clear blue sky.

"You can."

Fowler threw out his hands. "Name it."

"Who was on the case of the car that was pulled out of the harbor three weeks ago? Emilia García was the girl's name. The mother died."

Fowler gave me a puzzled look.

"I don't have time to explain," I said.

He shrugged. "All right, it was Detective Ferdinand."

"Got it," I said, then turned around and left, forgetting to shut the door behind me.

"You're welcome," Fowler yelled behind me, but I barely heard him.

I hurried down the hallway until I reached Ferdinand's desk. I had known the guy for ten years and worked on several cases with him. He was known to be a good detective and one I trusted.

"Hunter?" he asked and closed a drawer, looking

up at me from behind his reading glasses. Ferdinand was pretty much my opposite. Small and chunky, and standing next to my six-feet-eight, he looked almost like a child. He had a handsome face behind the glasses and kind eyes. He was around ten years older than my thirty-six years and had been in the force for twenty-five years. From his computer screen, his wife and two adult children looked back at him, smiling on a beach somewhere. He liked to work weekends so he could take time off during the week instead when his wife had to work.

"I thought this was your day off. You never work Sundays."

"It was. I need your help."

Ferdinand nodded toward the chair, signaling for me to sit down. I did, even though everything inside me screamed that I was running out of time.

"What's on your mind?"

"Emilia García."

"The girl we pulled out of the harbor?"

"That's her."

"What about her?"

"I need the details of the case."

Ferdinand nodded. He turned around and opened a drawer behind him, then looked for a few seconds before he pulled out a file that he placed on the desk in front of me.

"This is all there is on them as of now. It was pretty straightforward. The case was closed after three days."

Chapter 8

"IT WAS SUICIDE," Ferdinand said with an exhale. "They had been living on the streets for some time, sleeping in their car, and we figured the mom simply couldn't take it anymore and decided to end it for both of them. We found sleeping pills in the car, and the toxicology report stated that the mother had taken enough of the pills to knock out a small horse. We concluded that she popped a couple of pills, then ran the car over the edge, taking the daughter with her. Such a tragedy."

I stared at the file, flipping through the pages. "And the dad?"

Ferdinand bit his lip, then shook his head. "We never found him. They divorced two years ago, and he fell off the face of the earth."

"Do you have a name?"

"Luis Martìnez, a fairly common name. Right after we identified the mother, we sent a patrol out to his last known address, but they said he didn't live there anymore. They didn't know where he moved to. He might have left the country."

I nodded while looking through the pictures taken of the inside of the car. I paused at a picture of the mother.

"Have you looked for any other relatives? What about her parents?" I asked and tapped on the mother's picture. "Do you know anything about the grandparents? If the dad is nowhere to be found, they're the next of kin."

Ferdinand threw out his hands resignedly. "I know that she came down here from Dallas, Texas, so my guess is they're up there. I've spoken to Dallas PD and asked them to try and look for them, but that's all. I haven't heard anything. To be honest, I haven't had the time to dig deeper into it. You see this pile over here? All cases I have neglected over the past few months. I'm swamped here, Hunter. I simply don't have the resources to go chase down a father or a set of grandparents who may not even live in this state. No matter how much I want to."

I lifted my eyes and met his.

"Can I try?"

Ferdinand furrowed his eyebrows.

"Sure. I just don't seem to understand why. Why would you? Don't you have enough to do with the Four Seasons case?"

The Four Seasons case was the story of five men being found dead in a hotel room at the Four Seasons Hotel six days ago. I had been put on the case and had been buried in it for days. So far, it looked mostly like a drug deal gone wrong, but I had a feeling there was more to it than that. I just hadn't been able to break the case open yet. Everywhere I went, I was met with closed doors.

Today was Sunday, and I always take Sunday off to go to church with my family and then rest. I had been looking forward to this day. It was supposed to be a relaxing day with my family, and now it was turning out to be the most hectic day ever, trying to save my daughter's precious life.

I nodded. "I do. But this is something else. I'm not reopening the case, just trying to find the relatives."

"Be my guest," he said. "There was nothing I'd like more than to find the poor girl's relatives and let them know what happened. It would give final closure to this entire affair."

I grabbed the file and rose to my feet, sending Ferdinand half a smile.

"Thanks."

"If you succeed, then I'm the one thanking you," Ferdinand yelled after me as I hurried out to my motorcycle.

Seconds later, I was rushing across town toward the beach.

Chapter 9

"HUNTER? On a Sunday? This gotta be serious."

Al, alias Alvita, alias The Plague, opened the door and let me inside. I hurried past her, then put the file on her desk with the five monitors showing surveillance cameras from all over the world. I had never asked her what she used those for, or if it was even legal for her to be monitoring people in all those places. Some of them were obviously placed in people's homes, and others were in workplaces. We had an understanding. She helped me out, and I didn't ask any questions. Al was a former CIA hacker, and I had no idea how she made a living now. I wasn't sure I even wanted to. I had once helped find her sister's killer and earned myself a lifetime of services from her.

"It is," I said. "Josie is sick. I don't have time to

explain in more detail, but she needs a new heart asap."

Al looked at me from underneath her heavy dreadlocks. She was probably the shortest person I had ever known, but she still drew more attention to herself in a room than anyone I had ever met, even though she desperately didn't want to.

"And you think I have one?" she asked.

I shook my head. "No. There's a donor at the hospital, well maybe there is, but we need to find her relatives. She's a young girl who has been declared brain dead, but her heart is fine. She's a match, they say, but we can't find her family."

Al nodded. "I see. And you want me to find them?"

"Yes, please. I have the name of the dad."

She lifted her eyebrows. "A name? That's all?"

I grimaced. "I'm afraid so. The mother and the girl were homeless, living in their car. The parents are divorced. I have the last known address on the father, but he doesn't live there anymore."

Al nodded pensively while rubbing her dreadlocks that were pulled back into a thick ponytail. "All right, an address is good. We're starting to get somewhere. What about the mother. Did she have a phone?"

"She did, but it was destroyed in the water."

She looked at me, startled. "The water?"

"The mother and daughter drove into the harbor

three weeks ago. Suicide. The daughter survived but is brain dead; the mother died."

"And the phone wasn't waterproof?" she asked.

I shook my head. "I asked down in forensics, and they said it was completely destroyed. It was an old one."

Al's face lit up. She grabbed the file and opened it. "But if there was a phone, there is a phone record with a provider somewhere. Let me see what I can do. There's coffee in the pot in the kitchen. It's bulletproof coffee, but you don't mind, right?"

"Any coffee will do," I said, even though I wasn't very fond of Al's health keto power coffee since the fatty butter always threw me off a little. I had to admit, though, that it did give me extra energy from my first sip, and I needed just that. I sat on her red velvet couch that looked like something my grandmother would have in her living room, then tapped impatiently on the side of my cup as I drank, watching Al do her magic. I tried my best to pretend like I wasn't counting the minutes anxiously.

Chapter 10

"CAN I GET YOU ANYTHING?"

Jean looked at Josie in the bed. The girl looked so weak and pale; it was awful. Josie was usually such a strong girl, and Jean had never seen her like this.

Josie smiled feebly. "How about a new heart?"

Looking at her brought tears to Jean's eyes. She tried to stifle them since she didn't want the girl to see them.

"Your dad is working on that one," she said and took Josie's hand in hers. Harry's dad had been with her all afternoon but had just gone out for a coffee and a bite to eat. Jean felt worry in the pit of her stomach, gnawing at her insides. It tormented her to see Harry and Josie in this type of distress.

It had been a month since Camille had woken up, and Jean had snuck out of the house to leave them alone for the reunion. It wasn't without some pain that Jean had seen Camille come back to life. She was thrilled that she had; of course, she was. Camille had been her best friend. And it was what was best for Josie and Harry. But while Camille was sick, Jean had fallen in love with Harry. She had tried desperately not to and fought every urge, but it had happened anyway. And now, she had to push her feelings away every time she saw him, and that was painful. She had avoided him at all costs, taking extra shifts at the hospital to keep herself busy and away from the house. Yet, she still found herself standing in front of their house at night when coming home from her evening shift, staring at the porch, wondering what they had been up to that day, if they were getting proper food to eat, or if Josie needed help with her Spanish. She was simply missing being a part of their lives. While Camille was sick, she had been over there constantly when off from work. She had taken care of Camille, changing her feeding tube, her catheter, and making sure she didn't get pressure sores. She had cooked for Harry and Josie and often Harry's dad—who lived right down the street—too. She had plunged in headfirst and gotten herself too involved with them. And now it was all over. It was like she had lost her family. And the worst thing was that she wasn't allowed to feel the way she did. She had to be happy for them; she had to be thrilled that their prayers had been answered. Heck, she had even prayed for Camille's recovery herself on many occasions. She really shouldn't be feeling this way, this deep pain.

Yet, she was.

And now they were all here again, in trouble, needing her assistance yet again, ripping open the old wounds.

It didn't feel fair.

"I know," Josie said hoarsely. She closed her eyes briefly and seemed to be dozing off, but then opened them again and looked at Jean, squeezing her hand.

"I missed you," she whispered.

At first, Jean stared at her, startled, thinking she might have heard her wrong, but then the girl repeated it.

"I missed you, and so did Dad. He just won't admit it."

Jean swallowed hard, pressing back the tears. She sniffled and touched Josie's cheek gently, fighting her tears.

"You rest now, sweetie. You need it," she said, her voice shivering. "You need it to keep you strong."

Chapter 11

"HA. That was a lot easier than I thought."

I looked up from my coffee cup. I had been staring into the black glistening substance for a few minutes, dreaming myself away while thinking about Josie and then—guiltily admitted—Jean. Seeing her again today had made my heart jump, even though I felt ashamed about it. I missed her terribly and was so glad she could be with us at a time like this when we needed her the most. I felt terrible for what I had done to her, for turning my back on her just when we were about to be more than just friends and neighbors. I had broken her heart, and now my excuses were no good. But what could I have done differently? My wife had woken up after three years in a vegetative state. I couldn't very well turn my back on her now. What kind of a person would that make me? It didn't matter what my feelings were for Jean. I was a husband and a father before anything.

"You found something?" I asked and stood to my feet.

"Not just something. I found him, the dad."

I hurried to her desk. "Really?"

"Don't look so surprised," Al said. "I am actually quite good at what I do."

"I know you are…it was just really fast."

"I went through the phone records and internet browsing on her phone, which the phone company registers, even though they'll tell you they don't. Here, I found out that the mother had an old Facebook account. There are a lot of Jennifer Garcías out there, so finding the right one was a lot easier this way. She didn't use her profile much and hadn't posted for years, but she did post pictures of her husband and daughter three years ago before they were divorced. And bam, here he is."

She clicked and showed me a picture of a man holding a child of about seven or eight years old.

"This is Luis Martìnez?" I asked and pointed at his face.

"Bingo. So, now that we know what he looks like, we just need to find him. I ran a face recognition program, and *ba-da-bing*, look what came up."

Al scrolled on her computer and then stopped. "He changed his name one year ago, about the same time he moved from the address we have. If your little detective friend had thought about looking into it, maybe digging a little deeper, he'd have easily found the court documents. His name is now David Smith, one of the most common American names you can find. Probably had a hard time finding work and changed his name to make it easier. Or he got himself in some trouble and needed to hide."

"David Smith?" I asked.

"And there's more," she said.

"I hoped you'd say that."

"He lives right here beachside. Here's his address. Now, just like there are a lot of Garcías and Martìnezes around here, there are also a lot of David Smiths, so finding him wasn't straightforward. I found pictures of him from surveillance cameras downtown, places he seems to frequent, based on how many times he appears on them, especially on the one from an ATM at his local bank. That way, I could narrow it all down to a radius, then I searched for David Smith in that area, and I found him. Here's his address."

I stared at Al. I could have kissed her at this moment. Instead, I gave her a big hug, even though I knew she wasn't someone who enjoyed physical contact much.

"Thank you, thank you, Al."

"No problem," she said and pulled away as I let her go. "Now, go find him and save Josie."

"Let me know if there's anything I can do for you in return," I said.

"Something might be coming up," she said. "But not now. Go!"

Chapter 12

THE ADDRESS LED me to a small unit on top of a Cuban restaurant. A woman of Spanish heritage opened the door, and I asked for David Smith. She gave me a suspicious glare before she stepped aside and let me in. I followed her down a small hallway with rooms on both sides. All of them had people sitting or standing in them and voices speaking, some yelling loudly. There was a TV on somewhere and kids playing. The condo was no more than two bedrooms, but there seemed to be three or four families living there.

"David?" the woman said as we walked into what would have been a kitchen, but with all the mattresses on the floor, looked more like a shelter.

A man looked up from the back of the room, and all eyes were on me now. I recognized the face from Al's computer screen, where I had seen him holding his daughter tightly. He seemed ten years older than in that picture.

The woman nodded in my direction, and David stared at me, his eyes loaded with suspicion. I knew most of these people could tell I was a cop from far away, and David sure looked like he smelled it on me.

"I'm here about your daughter," I said, trying to soften him up. "Emilia?"

It worked. His eyes grew tender, and his shoulders came down. He approached me quickly.

"Is there a place we can talk privately?" I asked.

He nodded and showed me out on the balcony, where he lit a cigarette and blew out smoke. By the way he looked at me, I could tell he knew I wasn't bearing good news.

He puffed his cigarette. "How do you know my daughter? You a cop?"

I nodded and leaned on the railing, looking down on the street. Music rose from the Cuban restaurant below.

"I am sorry…"

He stopped me, raising his hand and turning his head away. "Please, don't…"

"But I have to," I said. "We've been looking all over for you. It happened three weeks ago, and no one has been able to find…"

He turned to look at me. "Three weeks ago?"

"Yes, the police have been searching for you to tell you…"

He shook his head, then slammed his hand into the railing. He bit back tears and took a deep inhale of his cigarette.

"How…how did it happen?"

"It was suicide," I said. "She drove the car into the harbor with them both in it. She took pills first. Jennifer didn't survive, and…"

He held his breath. "And Emilia? She's alive?"

I swallowed. This was beyond hard. I tried not to put myself in his situation, but that was even more difficult because it could be me in a short while. The thought brought tears to my eyes.

"Yes, I mean, not really."

He smoked again, looking at me with confusion. "I don't understand. She's alive, or she's not?"

My eyes hit the ground below. "She is…but she's not. She's been declared brain dead, and she'll never wake up."

A sob emerged from his lips as he could no longer keep it together. He brought a hand to his mouth while his torso shook. I placed a hand on his shoulder and let him cry for a few seconds, fighting to keep it together myself.

"Can I…Can I see her?" he finally asked.

I nodded. "Let me take you there."

Chapter 13

SHE WAS PRACTICING HER VIOLIN. Still, it didn't help her escape the odd feeling that she'd had all day like someone was watching her. Savannah Hart was worried she might be going crazy. She had been a little paranoid lately and felt an unease deep down in the pit of her stomach. Not even being inside her own home could help her feel at ease, and that was puzzling to her. Savannah stopped playing and walked to the window, then looked outside. A car was parked on the other side of the road. Was someone inside it? Was that the person who was watching her?

Savannah took a deep breath, then closed the curtains tightly, shaking her head. No, it was crazy. Besides, she had to practice for her concert next week. Savannah played in the Miami Symphony Orchestra and had since she was nineteen.

During the day, she was a music teacher at the local elementary school. It was a job she enjoyed more than anything. Giving away her joy of string music to the young ones was a privilege.

Savannah didn't have any children of her own and was never going to. Cancer had forced the doctors to remove her uterus when she was fifteen, and that put an end to that dream. It was a great sorrow for Savannah to know she'd never be a mother, and she had devoted herself to her strings instead, making that her passion.

She had barely begun playing her music again when her phone rang. She grumbled and picked it up. It was—of course—her mother. Just checking in, as usual, three or four times a day, depending on her level of paranoia. She had been like this ever since Savannah had been diagnosed with cancer as a teenager. She was constantly terrified that Savannah would drop dead, or worse, get kidnapped or killed in the big city.

"Hi, Mom," she said with a sigh.

"Oh, good, you're home," her mother said, her worried voice vibrating. "I thought you'd call as soon as you got home from work."

"Well, I forgot. I needed to practice. Besides, we spoke this morning, remember? You told me to check the romaine lettuce in my fridge and throw it out if it was from California where they had found E Coli."

"Yes, well, did you? Lots of people have gotten sick from this lately. You really should be careful."

"Mom, I don't even have romaine lettuce in my fridge."

Savannah closed her eyes tiredly. It was on days like these she wanted to leave the country and move to some small island somewhere, where they had no phones, where it could just be her playing her violin and nothing else. She was sick of having to deal with her mother every day like this. She constantly worried. It was probably all her concern that had made Savannah paranoid and feeling like she was being watched all the time.

It was exhausting.

"Listen, Mom, I gotta go."

"Oh, really? You haven't lit any candles, have you? I just read that the fumes are toxic…"

"Goodbye, Mom. I need to practice. I'm sure I'll talk to you later."

She hung up with a deep sigh, then rubbed her forehead. She put the violin back up on her shoulder, then closed her eyes and disappeared into her music, trying to get that feeling of unease to leave her body by playing it away.

Chapter 14

"SO, she's basically just lying there and can't do anything at all? She can't even hear me?"

David stood by his daughter's bedside and looked down at her, shaking his head. Doctor Scott had come in with us.

"I'm afraid not, Mr. Smith," he said. "There has been no brain activity detected over the past three weeks, and she has been declared brain dead. That means her brain is no longer working in any capacity and never will again. I am sorry."

David touched her arm gently, running a finger up against the skin. "She's grown so much, you know? I can't believe how tall she's gotten. She looks just like her mother now."

He wiped his nose with his hand, then sniffled, pushing back more tears, looking at the ceiling.

"I never should have left them. I don't know what I was thinking. I thought…I thought it was best for them. You know what I mean?"

I nodded like I did.

"Me and Jen, we were…fighting every day, and I thought they'd be better off without me. I was in no state to take care of them. I got in with the wrong group and I…well, I feared for their lives, for our lives. I didn't know that things were this bad. I didn't know they were sleeping in their car. I mean, when you first came to me, I thought maybe they had been in a car accident, or they had been shot or something. It was a bad neighborhood where we used to live. I hoped that if I left, the gangs would leave them alone. I owed money, you know? I got myself into a lot of trouble, and there was no other way out. I had to do it. I had to go into hiding. That's why I changed my name and left and have kept hidden for years, not even contacting my daughter on her birthdays and missing all the Christmases. I thought they were safe this way, at least from me and my problems. I didn't know they had lost the house and were living in a car. I didn't know they were in trouble. And I have to say; I never thought that she would…that Jen would…kill herself. She was such a survivor, you know? A true fighter. I've known her for fifteen years. She never struck me as someone who'd do that."

"Living in the streets, sleeping in your car can be

tough," I said. "She might have grown hopeless, not seeing another way out."

"Still…" he said, quietly looking down at Emilia. "I don't know why she'd do that, and do this to…to our daughter?"

"Depression and hopelessness can lead people to do things we never thought they'd be capable of," Doctor Scott said, then signaled for me to leave.

I walked outside the room, breathing raggedly, my heart breaking. The doctor began his chat with David while I closed the door and left them to it. I walked down the hallway, my heart sinking. I was fighting to keep the anxiety at bay. I stood in the hall, closing my eyes briefly, sliding down with my back against the wall, squatting while praying for the right results, praying that David would make the right decision.

This was the moment when Doctor Scott would speak to David about shutting off the girl's life-support and ask if he'd consider donating her functioning organs, and especially her heart. This was the moment my daughter's future would be determined.

David Smith held it all in his hands.

Chapter 15

ONLY A FEW MINUTES LATER, the door slammed open, and David Smith stormed out into the hallway. I rose to my feet and looked at him, heart hammering in my chest.

I didn't like the expression on his face.

"You want me to kill my daughter so you can save yours? Is that why you came to find me? You didn't think I'd figure that one out, did you?"

I swallowed hard while staring at the man in front of me. Then I nodded. I had told him about Josie before we drove to the hospital and how she was waiting for a donor heart. Of course, he would know it was for Josie when the doctor asked him to consider donating, even if he wasn't allowed to say who would receive the heart. David was many things, but stupid wasn't one of them.

"You're right," I said. "That is why I came looking for you. Because my daughter needed your help, but please understand. My daughter's life depends on her getting a new heart."

He snorted. "And so, you thought she could get my daughter's heart, huh? And tell me, why is your daughter more important than mine, huh? Why is her life worth more than Emilia's?"

"It's not…believe me, I never thought it was. But my daughter has a chance—a very small chance—of living, but only if she gets a new heart."

"How can you be so sure that my daughter doesn't? Do you know the future? Do you know what will happen tomorrow?"

"Of course, I don't."

"I know what the doctors say about her, about her being brain dead and all that, but do they really know for sure? I mean, there are always stories about people waking up, right? It could happen; it could be a miracle. How can you ask me to shut her off and deny me the possibility of a miracle happening?"

That hit me where it hurt. Who was I to say that God couldn't perform a miracle on the girl, even though the doctors had said it was impossible? Was I robbing Emilia of that opportunity? I had seen one happen in my own house. I had seen my wife come back from a condition they said she wouldn't.

David stared at me, nostrils flaring, then calmed himself. He gave me a compassionate look.

"Listen, man…I am sorry about your daughter; I really am. If anyone understands what you're going through, it's me right now. If I could give you any of my organs to save her, I'd do so willingly. But I can't do what you're asking me to. I simply can't. I am not going to kill her. I can't do it."

My heart dropped when hearing those words. I knew it had been a long shot from the beginning, but I had to admit, I had believed in it to the end. I had truly thought he would see the sense in saving my daughter.

"I understand," I said, my voice breaking.

He placed a hand on my back. "I'm sorry. I'm sure there is another heart out there for her."

I didn't look at him. I just turned around and walked away, trying to hide my tears. I wasn't angry with him. I truly wasn't. He was right. We didn't know tomorrow. We couldn't know for sure that something amazing wouldn't happen. Fact was, I knew I would have done the same. I, for one, believed in miracles and would never dare to take God's matters into my own hands. How could I ask him to do something I never would?

Chapter 16

MY DAD PROMISED to take care of Camille, so I could spend the night with Josie, holding her hand. She felt so weak and feeble, and her eyes were filled with concern as she looked at me.

"There'll be another heart, Dad," she said, speaking with a small, still voice. It was so typically Josie to worry more about me in this situation than herself. "I'm sure they'll find one in time. God won't leave me or let me die like this, and you know it."

I exhaled and smiled. I had to admit I admired her faith in this crucial moment and wished I could have just a piece of it, just enough to make it through the night. But the fact was, I was losing all my faith and with it my hope that things would end up all right. It was hard to believe in miracles when sitting and holding your dying daughter's hand, everything screaming inside of you.

Where are you, God? Why is this happening to me? Don't you care about me? You can't let her die. You can't let her die!

I held her hand in mine till she dozed off, then decided to go to the vending machine to quiet my screaming stomach. I had gotten some chocolate when an alarm suddenly sounded. I immediately glanced toward my daughter's room, only to see nurses rushing about.

Josie!

I dropped my chocolate bar and ran to her room. Inside, nurses were yelling, and the machines sounded like they were screaming.

"What's going on?" I asked.

"Please, stay outside," a nurse told me and closed the door.

I stared at the closed door, my heart sinking. I didn't even see Jean come running down the hallway. She came up to me, her face strained. She was holding papers in her hand that she held up in front of me.

"What's going on?" she asked, perplexed.

Tears sprang to my eyes. "I…I don't know. All the alarms went off and then…they told me to wait out here. I fear her heart has…"

Jean's eyes grew wide. "Oh, no."

She held the papers up so I could see them. I didn't understand.

"He signed them," she explained. "The consent forms. Doctor Scott left them in Emilia's room, and the dad signed them and left them in there. I came straight from there. I went to check on her vitals and saw that he was gone; her father was gone. On the table, he had left the papers and this note. It has your name on it."

She held the note up and showed it to me. It read:

IT'S ALL MY FAULT. I KILLED HER. I KILLED MY DAUGHTER. NOW YOURS WILL LIVE. TREASURE EVERY MOMENT YOU HAVE WITH HER.

I read it a few times to make sure I had read it right, then looked up at Jean. "So... that means…?"

She nodded. "That was why I came down here…to tell you that you got the heart. You got it, Harry. Josie has a new heart."

I stared at Jean and felt so confused. I didn't know what to think. Was Josie saved? Or was it too late?

That was when the door of Josie's room burst open, and she was rushed out on a stretcher and soon disappeared down the hallway. Jean followed them, leaving me behind, feeling completely helpless.

ONE MONTH LATER

Chapter 17

"DO WE HAVE ANY AVOCADO? I am in such a mood for avocado."

I turned to look at my daughter. Josie was out of her bed and sitting in the kitchen. She was getting bored with being at home all day long, and I was about ready to send her off to school again soon.

The school had been really great and understanding. They had let her do online school as much as she was capable, and luckily, she was a bright kid, so she'd catch up soon enough when she got back.

Her breastbone still wasn't entirely healed after the transplant, and we still had to keep a close eye on her incision wound, cleaning it often so it wouldn't get infected. Other than that, she seemed to be fit for fight. The first two weeks after the transplant, she was still weak and got tired really easy. But now she was my good old Josie with the big brown, gleaming eyes. She was slowly gaining weight again, even though she had to watch her diet to speed up the recovery and make sure she didn't eat too much fat and stayed with lots of greens. She was going to have to take medication for the rest of her life to make sure her body didn't reject the heart, but that was a small price to pay.

"Avocado?" I asked puzzled. "You don't like avocado. I never buy them because you hate them?"

Josie shrugged. She had taken her sketchbook out and was drawing some strange creature with only one eye. She had been into a lot of creepy stuff lately, and I figured it was a phase. Josie looked at her finished product, then turned the page and began a new drawing.

"Well, now I do," she said.

I dried my hands on a dishtowel. "I'll buy some when I shop later. They're good for your heart."

My boss, Major Fowler, had also turned out to be great through this time of hardship for me. He had let me work from home a lot while taking care of Josie. That, along with my dad's help, stepping in when I needed it, ensured I was able to manage through this past month.

I was still working on the Four Seasons' case and had to admit I hadn't gotten anywhere with it. Not that I wasn't trying; I guess my focus was just somewhere else these days. Not that anyone blamed me. I had dodged a major bullet here. No wonder all I wanted was to be with my daughter and enjoy still having her.

Meanwhile, Josie spent most of her time during the day sitting with her mother, talking to her. Camille still hadn't improved much, but she did say Josie's name often, sometimes repeating it several times in a row, other times yelling it out, and that made our daughter feel like she was listening to what she said. Even though we all knew it was the only word Camille could say and that it could mean a lot of things. It still made Josie feel like she was special to her mother.

Jean had started to stop by again regularly since the operation, and I liked that. She checked in on Camille and was bugging me about getting Camille to a rehabilitation center so she could start getting her legs and arms to function again along with her speech. I had been looking at a couple of places that were within my budget, but there was a waitlist. It would take a few months, they said. Once again, we'd have to be patient.

It was hard for me not to think about David Smith. Every time I looked at my daughter, I felt such profound gratefulness to the man, and it pained me that I didn't know where he was. I wanted to do something for him in return; I just didn't know what. What would make you feel better after doing something like this? Maybe it was more my desire than it was his because I felt awful that his daughter had to die for mine to live.

"Also, buy some root beer," she said while still drawing.

I paused. "Excuse me? Root beer?"

She looked up and nodded, mocking me. "Yes, root beer, Dad. You know…the sodas."

"I know what root beer is, but you hate root beer, remember?"

She gave me *that* look, the one only a teenage daughter can give you and get away with.

"Well, not anymore. Things are changing, Dad. Keep up."

And with that, she let go of her sketchbook and left me. I stood back, smiling. Just watching her walk up the stairs made my heart so happy. She was no longer out of breath easily, and she seemed to be growing stronger and stronger each day that passed. It was hard to believe that it was the same girl who had been so weak just a short while ago, lying in her hospital bed.

It had been the last minute, they said. Josie's body had given out right before Jean brought me the signed papers. They had told me afterward that her organs were shutting down . If David hadn't signed the papers when he did and Jean found them when she did, it would have been too late.

"God might not be early, but he is never too late," my dad had said. Once again, I had to say he was right. Even though I still struggled with the fact that it had to happen in the first place.

I walked to the kitchen table, grabbed her sketchbook, and was about to close it when I paused. I stared at the drawing Josie had made, puzzled. Not so much because of how good it was, that surprised me too since Josie wasn't usually very good at drawing because she was too impatient.

It was what she had drawn that made my blood run cold.

Chapter 18

I FLIPPED the pages in the book and looked at the previous drawings, then grabbed the sketchbook in my hand and walked up the stairs. I knocked on Josie's door, then walked inside.

"You forgot this downstairs," I said and held up the sketchbook.

"Oh, thanks," she said.

I opened it to the drawing that had gotten my attention. "What's this?"

She looked at it. "Oh, it's nothing."

"It must be something since you've drawn it several times. Look. It's the same scene over and over again. Where did this come from?"

"It's just this nightmare I keep having," she said with a sigh. "It's nothing, really. Calm down."

I looked at the sketch again. It showed a car in the

water, sinking into the harbor, and a little girl inside the car looking out the window.

"You're dreaming about this?" I asked.

"Yeah, almost every night."

"How long has this been happening?"

"Since I got back from the hospital, I guess, why?"

I shook my head. "No reason. I was just wondering."

I stared at the sketch again, my heart pounding in my chest. I had never told Josie about the girl whose heart she received…about Emilia. She couldn't possibly know that was how she died, could she? Had she heard it somewhere else? Maybe at the hospital? But only Jean would know that the heart came from Emilia. It was usually kept anonymous. And Jean would never tell her about Emilia. I couldn't imagine why she would.

"Who is she?" I asked, to figure out if she knew.

Josie shook her head with a shrug. "I told you. I don't know. Just someone from my dream."

I stared at the sketch, then back up at my daughter, wrinkling my forehead, wondering. How was this even remotely possible? How could she know the details about Emilia's death so well? The station wagon in the sketch was even painted a bright green like the real one had been, the one I saw in the case files.

"Why are you so interested in some silly dream anyway?" she asked with a scoff.

I ignored her remark. I couldn't stop looking at the

drawing, my pulse quickening. It wasn't just the details that spooked me. There was more to it than that. What had me totally freaking out was something else in the drawing, something—or someone—standing on the dock.

"Who is he?" I asked.

She exhaled. "I don't know who he is. It starts with me waking up inside the car, and it's moving, and then I look out the window and see him standing there, looking at me with these steel-gray eyes. I just know in that instant that he's the one who somehow made the car fall into the water."

Josie shivered as she spoke. I could tell it was unpleasant for her to talk about it, and I wondered if that was why she hadn't told me.

"It freaks me out every time," she added, "and then I usually wake up."

Chapter 19

I TOOK Camille out for a walk, pushing her in a wheelchair. She enjoyed getting outside and going for a stroll around the neighborhood, looking at the flowers. She pointed at a big red rose, and I pushed her close to it, then plucked it and gave it to her. She smiled at me, then started to cry.

"Oh, no, sweetie," I said and bent down. "Are you okay?"

Her head tilted sideways, while tears were still running down her cheeks.

I smiled and hugged her. "I know. I know. You can't help it. You can't control your reactions. We'll get you better soon, I hope."

I pushed her down the street, letting her cry while dangling the rose in her hand. I felt tears coming to my eyes as well while wondering if I would ever see the

Camille I had loved so dearly again. I was ashamed to admit it, but this didn't seem like her. This felt like a completely different person.

I stopped at a park so she could watch the children play while I sat on a bench next to her. Camille liked watching them play; at least, I believed she did. It was hard to tell. At least it was a change of scenery from the bedroom, and she had to enjoy that.

We looked at the young children playing while sharing a snack. She was eating better on her own now, and that was a huge improvement. I just wished I knew what was going on inside that mind of hers behind those beautiful eyes. If only I understood what she needed, what she wanted.

Did she still love me? Did she remember anything from our life together?

"Why did you do it?" I suddenly asked out of the blue. I hadn't planned on saying anything, but it had been on my mind for so long, it just burst right out of me. "Why did you start doing drugs again?"

I stared at her, feeling stupid. The woman couldn't speak a single sentence. What did I expect to get out of her? Maybe nothing. Maybe that wasn't why I asked. Maybe I just needed to get the words across my lips.

She lifted her glance, and our eyes locked. I stared into them, wondering if she even had understood the question at all.

She parted her lips, and a word left her lips.

"Josie."

It was pretty much the only word she had said since she woke up. That and *ba-ba*, which she said a lot too, but I had no idea what that meant yet either. The doctor had said there was damage caused to her speech, language, and swallowing, and it could take years for her to rehabilitate it all. I just hoped we could start her rehabilitation therapy soon. I hated that we'd have to wait.

Camille's face looked confused as she repeated the word "Josie."

I nodded and took her hand in mine.

"Yes, Josie."

But her eyes remained bewildered as she kept looking at me, barely able to lift her head enough to do so.

"Josie."

"Yes, Josie," I repeated.

She shook her head and looked like she was really trying to say something, then almost yelled out into the park:

"JOSIE!"

She was getting agitated now, and I took her hand in mine, trying to calm her. It was obvious that I had upset her with my question. She yelled it again, repeating it over and over:

"JOSIE! JOSIE! JOSIE!"

People were turning to look at us, concerned looks in their eyes, some even pulling their children away fearfully. I got up, smiling awkwardly at them, then started to push her back toward the house while she still kept yelling our daughter's name.

Chapter 20

"SHE WAS YELLING, YOU SAY?"

Jean looked at me over the steaming cup of coffee. After my walk with Camille, I had put her back to bed, where she had finally calmed down and fallen asleep. I needed to get out, so I walked next door and knocked. Jean served us coffee and a piece of chocolate pie she had baked that smelled divine. Two of my favorite things were chocolate and pie.

"Yes, everyone was staring, and I couldn't get her to stop. I feel terrible for admitting this, but I was really embarrassed. I can't stand seeing her like this. I hate to say it, but it's almost like it's worse than when she was just a vegetable, you know? Now, she's awake, but not much has changed, really. I still can't communicate with her, and I can see that she is trying to."

"It sounds like she was trying to tell you something,

and the words just wouldn't come; her brain wouldn't cooperate. I've seen it before in patients who suffered brain injury. I think she might be trying to tell you something. Maybe you need to give her some time, and then it'll come."

She sipped her cup, and I mine while feeling awful in my stomach. Had Camille sensed I was embarrassed about her? Had she simply been frustrated because I didn't understand her? Was that why she was yelling?

I shook my head. "I'm sorry for coming here like this. You must think I'm…"

"No," she said, placing her hand on my arm. "I am glad to be here for you. For all of you. You know I am."

I looked up, and our eyes met. On another day, in another lifetime, I'd have leaned over and kissed her in this instant. Instead, I pulled my arm away and leaned back.

"There's something else on your mind, isn't there?" Jean said. "I know you, Hunter. Something is going on in there. What is it?"

I exhaled. Jean knew me so well.

"It's Josie."

She sipped more coffee and ate her pie.

"What about her? Is she having trouble?"

I leaned forward, at first debating if I wanted to tell her this, then decided if anyone would understand and wouldn't laugh at me, it was Jean.

"She started having these dreams. Ever since she

got the new heart, she's made drawings of them. It scared me half to death, to be honest."

She gave me a look. "Why?"

"Because they showed how Emilia died."

Jean put the fork down on the plate. "Her donor?"

I nodded. "Yes. You know how her mother drove the car into the water down at the harbor. She's drawing that, and I don't know where she got the information. I haven't told her how Emilia died, have you?"

Jean shook her head. "I couldn't see why I or anyone would tell her that."

"And there's more in the picture than what we know, and that's what has me puzzled, to put it mildly."

"What is it?"

"A man. There's a man standing on the port, up on the dock, looking down at them. Josie says he's always standing there in the dream, and he scares her. She also says that he somehow made the car fall in the water."

"I see," Jean said. "And now you're worried that maybe it wasn't a murder-suicide, that it was, in fact, something else, am I right?"

I nodded.

"I fear they were both murdered, yes."

Chapter 21

"I JUST CAN'T UNDERSTAND how on earth Josie would know about this. That's what I'm struggling with," I said and sipped more coffee. "I mean, if I choose to believe this, to believe that they were actually murdered, then what do I do next? I can hardly reopen the case based on my daughter's dreams, can I? They'll all think I've gone nuts. More than usual."

Jean thought it over for a few seconds.

"It's actually not that uncommon. There have been lots of reports of organ transplant receivers claiming they seem to have inherited the memory, experiences, and emotions of their deceased donors, even though they never knew anything about them. I know they did a huge research project recently where a doctor found sixty-something transplant patients and collected their accounts. He wrote an entire book about it, which I read; I just don't recall the title. But it was quite stunning how they had changed in personality, and how they carried memories that, when it was researched, turned out to have belonged to their donors. A woman who had never liked beer started to drink beer and eat green peppers and chicken nuggets suddenly after receiving a heart from an eighteen-year-old man. She kept dreaming about him too and knew his name was Tim and ended up going looking for him. Others say they have suddenly developed a taste for classical music…stuff like that. There was also a girl who was gay before the heart transplant, and after, she wasn't. I think I have the book here somewhere," she said and got up. She walked to the living room, then came back with a book between her hands.

"This is the one." Jean opened it to a page. "Here's one that is very similar to Josie's story. This is a woman who says that she dreams about her donor's accident every night. She says she can feel the impact in her chest as the car slams into her. She also says she hates meat now, even though she loved it before. Here, you can take the book home and read it if you like."

Jean slid the book to me across the table.

I stared at her, then down at the book in front of me.

"So, it's really a thing?"

"Yes, Harry. You're not going crazy, and neither is Josie. The theory behind this phenomenon is that memory is accessible or processed through the cells, and since the heart possesses cells similar to the brain, and it has been proven that the heart sends information to the brain, it may be possible that information about memories and traits may be transferred to the recipient's brain."

"So, let me get this straight," I said. "You're telling me that heart transplant recipients can receive information through the donor's heart after it has become part of their body?"

"That's the theory, yes," she said, "but read the book and you'll know more. I found it very interesting."

Jean looked at her watch.

"Anyway, I should get to work. I have the evening shift tonight."

I left her house and walked back to mine, book in my hand. I made myself another cup of coffee, then sat with the book in the living room, reading through all the accounts, one after another, startled and pushed in my beliefs of what was possible for the human body. I had to admit, it all made a lot more sense: the sudden cravings for avocadoes and root beer, her sudden ability to draw, and her new-found interest in creepy stuff that she had never had before.

It all made so much more sense.

But it also meant that, if this was true, if what Josie was dreaming actually happened, then somewhere out there was a murderer who had killed Emilia and Jennifer García, and who was getting away with it.

Chapter 22

THE RAIN DRUMMED on the roof of the car and poured on her windshield so hard the wipers almost couldn't keep up. It was a typical Florida afternoon thunderstorm, and it always clogged the traffic through downtown. People slowed down, some almost till they came to a stop, and now Savannah was barely moving forward.

She looked in her rearview mirror at the car behind her to make sure it kept its distance. In the back, she had her case with her violin. She had been at practice with the orchestra, and now she felt tired. It had been a long day. The kids at school had been impossible. They were so loud, and their instruments sounded awful. There was especially one kid who always gave her trouble. His name was Jarrett. As usual, he hadn't practiced for today and kept stopping when they just got into it.

He was the only one in class who played the double bass, and that meant he had to know his stuff; otherwise, he threw them all off.

Savannah finally reached the intersection where she had to turn to get to her small street, then drove down the wet road through the puddles. As she parked the car in front of her townhouse, she looked in the rearview mirror again and thought she saw the same car that had been behind her all the way home.

Savannah turned her head to look, but the car continued past her, accelerating down the street, where it took a turn at the end.

"That was odd," Savannah said and wrinkled her nose. She could have sworn she had seen the same car parked outside her house several times this week. Was it following her? Was someone watching her?

You're being paranoid again. You're turning into your mother.

She walked inside and put down her case. She hung her keys on the hook, then walked into the kitchen, where she grabbed herself some water that she drank while looking into the street. She didn't like it. It had been going on for weeks now, this paranoia, this feeling of constantly being watched.

Maybe she should see someone about it?

Except there was something that made her think she wasn't completely off, that it wasn't her going crazy. She knew she had a reason to be cautious, a reason to fear for her life.

Because of what she knew. Because of what she had seen.

Savannah shook her head in distress. She didn't like to even think about it. It made her so anxious, it almost hurt. Yet, as she stood there in her kitchen, she couldn't help herself. No matter how much she tried, she couldn't escape the images in her mind…images of the man with the steel-gray eyes and big hands. Of the dead body on the ground. Of the blood on the ground.

Savannah dropped the glass she was holding. It slid out of her grip and fell onto the tiles below, where it shattered. Small pieces of glass were everywhere, and she began to clean them up but cut her finger on one of them. She stared at the blood from the tip of her finger, while images of the body and the blood on the ground flashed through her mind, making her lose her balance. She reached over for the kitchen table and closed her eyes, trying to replace the images with something nice, something pleasant.

She looked over at the violin case, then wiped the blood off on a paper towel, opened the case, and took out her beloved violin. She touched it gently, then took out the bow and placed it on the strings.

She closed her eyes and started to play, drifting off into the world of music. She played like this for hours and hours on end, not even realizing it had become dark out and nighttime was fast approaching. Savannah kept playing, pressing her tears and fears back till her fingers hurt, and she had no more strength in her arms to hold the violin.

Then she finally put the violin down with a loud exhale. She slid into a kitchen chair, thinking she ought to feel hunger, but she didn't. She was too upset, too exhausted for that.

As she decided to call it a night and turned off the lights in the kitchen and walked to the stairs, she heard a noise coming from behind her. She gasped and looked toward the back entrance leading to the yard. A shadow was standing there, wearing a raincoat. The water from his jacket was dripping on the floor.

Chapter 23

I WAS UP MOST of the night reading the book Jean had given me, taking notes along the way. There was so much of what these patients said that was similar to what I had experienced with Josie. Mostly the small quirky changes in personality. Yet, I was still skeptical and not completely ready to cry bloody murder. Josie could, after all, somehow have heard about the child and mother being pulled out of the water at the port before she had her heart failure…before she got the heart from Emilia. It happened three weeks before the heart transplant, and she could have seen it on TV or read about it online. Maybe she had even forgotten that she had heard about it.

I did some research online and read up on the details that had been told in the newspapers and on TV from when the car was found in the water. No one had witnessed it drive into the water, but someone at the port, working on a container ship close by, had heard the splash and seen the roof as it went down. He had called nine-one-one, and they had sent in divers to pull Emilia and her mother out. But no one had seen it go in.

At least no one that had come forward.

I dozed off at around three a.m., reminding myself to get some work done on my Four Seasons case the next day. Fowler had called earlier and left a message, asking me how things were progressing. I hadn't called him back because I didn't have any news to tell. The case hadn't been on my mind much lately, but I knew I had to get back to it soon, or Fowler would get in one of his moods and start talking about taking me off it. I needed to prove my worth to him, and that I was still one of the team. It wouldn't be long before Josie would be back in school, and then I'd be able to get back to work properly. Camille wasn't as dependent on me anymore, and she could easily spend the hours alone while I went to work. My dad said he'd be able to take her to therapy every day once she started.

I was dreaming of seagulls for some reason, seagulls hovering about my head, trying to grab food from my hand when I heard the scream. I opened my eyes with a gasp, then jumped out of bed and ran to Josie's room.

Inside, I found Josie sitting up in bed, lights on. She

had pulled the covers up over her head, and she was shaking badly.

"Josie? What's going on? Did you have another nightmare?"

I sat on the edge of the bed. She didn't answer, just kept trembling. I pulled her covers off, then pulled her into a hug. I held her in my arms, caressing her hair.

"My heart, Dad, it's racing so fast."

"Shhh, it's gonna be okay, sweetie. It was just a dream."

Josie shook her head. "N-no, Dad. This wasn't just a dream. You don't get it. This was…so real."

"Was it the one where you're inside the car again?" I asked. "The one from the drawings where the car ends up in the water?"

She shook her head. "No. This one was different. Completely different."

I nodded. "Okay, and what was it about then?"

She looked up at me, her eyes wide and scared. "A…It was a body, Dad. A body lying on the ground. There was a shot, a loud bang…actually, three of them, and then…there was this guy on the ground with blood around him."

"Okay? And then what?"

"That's it. I…I think I know where it happened. I think I know where the body is buried. There was a hole in the ground. Someone had dug a hole."

"Excuse me?"

She looked down like she was certain I wouldn't believe her. "I think it's real, Dad. I have this feeling..."

I didn't know what to tell her. Did I say that she was nuts? That her mind was playing tricks on her? Or did I indulge her? What if what she was seeing was, in fact, real like the people in the book? Many of them had seen actual events in their donor's lives, things that turned out to have actually happened.

Was this what it was?

There was only one way to find out.

"Get dressed," I said and threw a shirt at her.

"Why?"

"We're going for a little drive."

Chapter 24

JOSIE'S HANDS were clenched tightly around the coffee cup from Starbucks. We had stopped at a drive-through for a couple of necessary lattes and chocolate croissants to help keep us awake. Bugs were dancing in the beam from our headlights of the Chevrolet given to me by the city. I could tell Josie was uncomfortable doing this, but I still thought it was the best thing to do.

We had to know.

"Take a right over there," she said and pointed.

She had told me she didn't know the address of the place from her dream, but she knew exactly where it was.

I drove up in front of the City of Miami Cemetery, and she asked me to stop the car. I looked at the sign above the entrance in front of me.

"Here?"

She nodded. “Yes. I remember that sign from my dream. Come.”

I got out of the car and followed my daughter as she walked up to the pavement and continued toward the entrance to the cemetery. She stopped by the bars and the closed gate.

“It’s locked,” she said.

“Of course, it’s locked. Cemeteries are locked at night,” I said. “Says here, it closes at ten.”

She turned to look at me. Her eyes were gleaming in the light from the streetlamp above. A mosquito bit me on the neck, and I slapped it.

“In my dream, the gate was open when the man was killed. He was shot in the head and fell to the ground, limp as one of those rag dolls. We need to get in there.”

I pulled the large gate. “But we can’t, Josie. We’ll have to come back later.”

She shook her head. “No, Dad. I remember it now. I have it fresh in my memory exactly where the hole had been dug in the ground and where the man was shot. We have to do it now. We’ll climb the fence. It’s not that hard, see?”

She grabbed the bars and started to climb, pulling herself upward.

“Josie,” I said. “This is too hard for you. You have to be careful with your heart; you know this. No strenuous activity.”

"I'm fine, Dad, look," she said as she reached the top of the fence, then jumped down on the other side. I watched her hit the ground, my heart nearly stopping at the sight of her flying through the air and landing in the grass on the other side.

"Are you okay?" I asked.

She rolled to the side. "Yes, I'm fine."

"And your heart? Is it okay?"

"It's fine, Dad. Geez."

"Okay, I'm coming in after you."

I grabbed the bars and started climbing. I jumped down on the grass, then helped Josie get to her feet again.

"I'm fine, Dad, really. I feel fine. You're doing that worrying thing again."

"Okay, just let me know if you feel faint or lightheaded or anything out of the ordinary, okay? Shortness of breath? This is important."

I looked around us and into the dark cemetery. A sea of old tombstones was surrounding us.

"Okay, and where do we go next?"

She pointed.

"Right over here, come."

Chapter 25

"HERE," she said and showed me the place, lighting it up with the flashlight on her phone. The beam slid over a tombstone.

"*Timothy Wilson. Beloved father and husband?*" I said, reading from it. "This looks like a normal burial place, Josie."

"I know," she said. "But I remember this stone from my dream. I was watching…she turned around and let the light shine on a stone behind us. "From over there, covered by that tombstone, hiding behind it. I remember my hands were shaking. I also remember hearing my ragged breath. I remember being scared," she said and pointed with the light at the ground where I was standing. "Someone was standing here, and another man was with him. Then the first man pulled out a gun and shot him in the head. Three times. *POP*-

POP-POP. I saw him fall to the ground, dead in a pool of blood. Next to where you're standing, there was a big hole."

"But this guy, Timothy Wilson was eighty-eight," I said. "He died in two thousand and one."

"Look at the ground," she said and lit up the burial ground.

I knelt by it. I had to admit; the grass seemed very new on the grave. Much fresher than on the graves surrounding it, even though some of them were newer. There was also more dirt on it than the others. The grass was only partially covering the area.

It looked like it had been dug up not too long ago.

Josie knelt next to it, then dug her fingers into the dirt.

"What are you doing, Josie?" I asked.

She kept digging dirt up and moving it to the side.

"Help me," she said.

I looked around us, feeling sweat prickle on my face. If I were caught here, it wouldn't look good.

"This is vandalism, Josie," I said. "Timothy Wilson's family has paid for this place, for their beloved father and husband to rest in peace. You can't just dig up a random grave."

"Well, I don't care," she said. "I know what I saw is true, and I need to prove it to you. And to myself. Help me or not; I need to see what is down here under this dirt."

I stared at her, contemplating whether I should yell at her and drag her home like a good father would at this point.

But something held me back…the part of me that wanted to know too.

"Josie, you have to stop. Stop it now," I said. "You're gonna get us both arrested, and I could lose my job."

"Then help me so it'll be done faster," she said, panting agitatedly as she removed a huge chunk of dirt. I didn't like her working herself this hard. She had to be careful and preferably be in bed, not out digging holes in some cemetery at night. This wasn't good. This wasn't good at all.

"Josie," I said, exhaling, then knelt next to her and dug my fingers into the soft dirt as well.

Twenty minutes later, we had dug a small hole and were sweating like crazy.

"We're not getting anywhere without a shovel," I said, wiping my forehead with the back of my hand. "Maybe we should just call it quits."

"No," Josie said and continued. She dug in deep and pulled out a lot of dirt. Then, she stopped moving.

"What's wrong?" I asked.

"I think I touched something," she said. She reached down and pulled away more dirt when something came to light. Josie's face lit up, then her eyes turned terrified.

"I told you."

She kept digging till the arm was completely free from the dirt, and soon I helped her dig a body out till the torso and waist were visible, and we could pull it the rest of the way out of the ground.

I let the light shine on the face, or what was left of it. Maggots were crawling in the empty eye sockets, and the body had started to liquefy like they tended to if they'd been in the ground in a wet environment for more than a month. Still, I could easily tell who it was, and as I realized it, my heart dropped.

Chapter 26

IT WAS the ring on his finger that gave him away: a golden ring with a blood-red stone on the finger of his right hand, or the little that was left of it. I stared at the ring as the crime scene techs removed it from the bones and secured it for evidence, my heart sinking.

I had looked at that very ring so many times in my life when I had been in this man's office. The mere thought brought tears to my eyes.

"Hunter!"

I turned and spotted Fowler as he came up toward me. The crime scene techs had put up lamps to light up the area, and I could see his face clearly. He held an evidence bag up with something inside it.

"They found his wallet," he said. "It was in the jacket he was wearing when buried. It's him, no doubt."

I was the one who had called Fowler to tell him of our find. I thought he deserved to be the first to know. After all, he had known our former Major Wolfe better than any of us. Fowler had been Wolfe's protégé, and his only natural successor once he retired eight years ago. Those two were like family. Heck, we all were. But those two had been closer than any.

"I am sorry," I said. "I am so sorry."

Fowler paused. He, too, was fighting to keep it together. He bit his lip excessively while looking at the body.

"Yeah, well…" He stopped and gazed up at me. "You know how it is."

I nodded. "I didn't even know he was missing. Had you heard anything?"

Fowler rubbed his stubble. "Yvette called me about two weeks ago. She told me they had split up a few months earlier and that she hadn't heard from him in a while. He didn't pick up when she called, and she needed some stuff from the house. I figured he was angry at her and told her to keep it cool for a little while. I knew the divorce would have been hard on him; you know how much he worshipped Yvette."

I nodded. I did. She had been his everything. Yvette was French, and he had met her in Paris when they were both in their twenties. They had moved to Miami due to his career. But Yvette didn't like Florida. She didn't enjoy the lack of culture and history, as she put it, and she never grew fond of us Americans. Those two fought like cats and dogs, yet I always thought they loved each other deeply. It seemed like it. But apparently, it hadn't been enough after all.

"Anyway…" Fowler said. "I never followed up on it. I tried to call him once but then forgot about it. It never occurred to me that something might have happened to him. And especially not…this."

I nodded.

"So, what's your take on it?" he asked, nodding toward the remains of our former boss.

I swallowed and took a deep breath. "Burying his body on top of another grave is a clever way to make sure no one notices. Few people actually stop to look at the grave, especially when the guy is old and has been dead for a long time. Most people won't notice the new grass or that the dirt has been dug up. That's why the killer believed it was okay to leave the ring and wallet there…because he assumed Wolfe would never be found in a place like this. Three very distinct holes in the skull tell me he was shot three times in the head. I'd say it was an act done in sudden anger."

Fowler looked at the body and the crime scene techs who were taking photos and video of the scene. He then nodded.

"And you still stick to the story that it was Josie who led you out here?" he asked. "That she dreamt this because of her new heart?"

I nodded. "I know it's hard to believe, but as I told you, according to the book I read about this, it's been known to happen before. Earlier cases are very similar to what she's experiencing."

"I still don't quite buy it," he said. "But you did find the body."

"I'd also like to look into the death of Emilia and Jennifer García," I said, knowing I was overstepping here. But I had to give it a go. "Josie says she believes they were murdered."

Fowler chuckled and shook his head. "I think you have enough on your plate as it is. I can't have you chasing ghosts. I'm not reopening the case because your daughter had some weird dream about the girl who gave her a new heart. Come on, Hunter. How would I ever explain it to my superior? Everyone would think I had gone nuts. The case is closed, and you should let it go too. I know you cared for Wolfe, but you're too involved in all this. I'll have Ferdinand take this one."

I bit my lip, repressing my desire to get angry with him.

"Let it go," Fowler said and placed a hand on my upper arm. "For your own sake and Josie's."

The way he said it, it almost sounded like a threat, and it threw me off. Fowler was gone before I could confront him about it.

Chapter 27

I KNOW I was supposed to be doing something else. I was supposed to be working on a different case. Yet, there I was, defying all orders from my boss by being at the police impound, showing my badge to the guy at the window along with an evidence number I had taken from the García case file.

"Yeah, I know that one," the guy behind the glass said and got up from his chair. "It's right over here. Follow me."

I did, and we walked through a carpark of impounded cars. Cars that had been parked in wrong places, cars that had been held back for evidence, and cars rusting away because no one knew what else to do with them.

He stopped by a rusty old green Ford Escort station wagon that looked like it had been young in the late nineties. The type you just didn't see on the roads anymore. Rust was eating it up, and it hadn't helped that it had been submerged underwater before being pulled out with two people inside of it.

Two people my colleagues assumed had killed themselves. Two people I had a feeling had been murdered.

"There she is," the guy said. "Not much left of her, though."

"It's all I need," I said. "Thank you."

The guy gave a sniffle, then left me.

I stared at the old rusty car, while a million questions welled up in my mind. There was so much I needed answers for that I hadn't gotten from reading through the case file. There was especially one thing I believed they hadn't examined. Was the front door locked? No matter how much I had read through the files, it didn't say anywhere. When they pulled it out of the water, did they have to break a window to get the bodies out? It didn't say that either.

I reached over and grabbed the front door, then pulled it open. It sure wasn't locked now. And no windows had been broken. Had the divers been able simply to open the front door and pull them both out?

And what about the keys? Had they been in the ignition? It didn't say in the report, but they weren't there now. I grabbed the case file in my hand and flipped through the pages, looking for my answer. And there it was, right in front of me in black and white in the forensics report.

The keys were found inside the mother's jacket.

"How do you drive an old car like this one with the key in your pocket?" I mumbled and looked inside. I knelt by the driver's seat and looked under the steering wheel. Two small wires were sticking out, and as an old Miami cop, I knew exactly what that meant.

The station wagon had been good old-fashioned hotwired.

I took a photo with my phone, then leaned inside and took a few more of the inside, while wondering about another thing, the very thing that had me puzzled from the first time I read the report.

I then grabbed my phone and called Detective Ferdinand.

"Yes?"

"How come they were in the back seat when they were found?"

"What are you talking about?" he asked.

"The García files. It says in there that they were both pulled out from the back of the station wagon that had been arranged like a sleeping area because they lived in the car. It says both the mother and daughter were in the back when pulled out. Wouldn't the mother at least be in the front if she drove the car into the harbor?"

Ferdinand sighed on the other end. "You've got to

be kidding me. Of all the days, you choose today to bother me with this? Do you have any idea how busy we are right now with what you found last night?"

"I am very well aware," I said, not backing down. I demanded answers now. "But this is important too."

"All right, all right," he said. "I guess they were pushed back. That's what one of the forensics techs suggested, that the mother could have been pushed back by the water when they went in."

"What if that's not what happened?" I said, staring at the station wagon in front of me. "What if someone broke into the car and hotwired it, then drove it to the edge, got out, and pushed it into the water?"

Ferdinand exhaled. "Listen, Hunter. I don't have time for this. They were two homeless people; they drove into the harbor either to commit suicide or maybe by accident because the mother had taken drugs. I don't know. But I do know the case is closed, and I suggest you leave it that way if you know what's best for you and your family."

With that, he hung up, and I stood back, feeling like I had once again been threatened by someone I thought I knew well.

What the heck was going on here?

Chapter 28

JEAN HAD BROUGHT Camille into the kitchen and had her sitting in her chair. Harry had bought her a brand-new wheelchair, one that supported her head, so she could lean back now and then when she needed to rest or couldn't hold it up properly herself.

Camille looked up at her, then smiled, using only one side of her mouth. It was all the gratitude she was capable of showing; Jean knew that much. She handed her a fork, then placed the cut-up meat in front of her and sat down. Camille struggled to put the fork into a piece of meat and missed a few times.

Josie was there too and stared at her mother while she fought to get just one piece of meat into her mouth.

"It's crazy, right?" Jean said when seeing the sadness in the girl's eyes. "How she has to learn everything from scratch again. Learn how to walk, how to eat, and one day, hopefully, talk again. But she's making progress every day. I haven't been here in a while, so I can really see the difference."

Josie nodded, biting her lip. Jean could tell a lot was going on in the poor girl's mind. It couldn't be easy to see her mother like this.

"Will she ever be the same, the way she was before?" she asked.

Jean sighed and helped Camille guide the fork closer to another piece of meat. "Probably not exactly the same," she said. "But she can get close."

"It just takes so long," Josie said.

It was Harry who had asked Jean to stay with Josie for a few hours today while he was at work. He didn't want Josie to be left alone in the house with Camille after what they had discovered the night before. He felt she needed to be with an adult, and his father, old Pastor Bernard, was out of town for the day. Jean still felt a little strange being back in the house, and with Camille now being aware of her surroundings. It had destroyed her chances of ever being with Harry, but she was still happy for them that they had gotten their mother and wife back…or at least some version of her, that was.

Jean reached out and grabbed Josie's hand in hers, then smiled warmly.

"Give her time. I know it seems like it's going slowly but think of her as a baby who has to learn everything.

It takes time. But I think she can do it. Your mom is strong."

Jean looked at Camille, realizing she actually didn't know how much Camille understood. She didn't seem to be listening to what they were saying, but there was a tear in her eye that rolled down her cheek. Jean wiped it away with a tissue, then squeezed Camille's hand as she let go of the fork, and it fell to the plate with a loud clang.

"Are you tired, Camille?" she asked. "You look tired. I think it's time for your afternoon nap. Here, let me help you with…"

She grabbed the napkin she had placed under her chin and tried to wipe Camille's mouth with it, but Camille turned her face away and gave Jean a push. She then let out a wail of sorts, sounding like a wounded animal.

"What's happening?" Josie asked.

"I think she's upset."

"Was it something I said? Was it because I said I thought it was taking too long, because I didn't mean it, Mom. I'm just happy to have you back, really."

Camille stared at them, shaking her head and torso violently from side to side.

"I think I'll take you to your room to get that nap," Jean said.

She grabbed the chair and rolled Camille to the small bedroom in the back that used to be Harry's office, but now was the room Camille slept in, so they didn't have to get her up and down the stairs. Just till she could walk them on her own, which Harry believed wouldn't be long. Jean helped Camille get into bed, then put the covers on top of her and held her hand in hers while squeezing it.

"I know you're in there, Camille, and I want you to keep fighting, okay? For Harry and Josie. They need you to get well. I know you can do this, Camille. You don't get to give up, do you hear me?"

Camille lay still with her eyes open for a little while and groaned like she was trying to speak. It was something she did a lot. Earlier in the day, Jean had tried to hand her a pencil and a paper, thinking she might be able to write what she wanted to say, but so far, Camille hadn't been able to hold the pencil still enough to write anything. If only there were some way for them to communicate.

"It'll come," Jean said. "The words. Just be patient, okay?"

With that, Camille closed her eyes and started breathing heavier. Jean rose to her feet and walked to the window to close the curtains when she spotted a car with someone sitting inside it on the street across from them and realized it had been there all morning.

Chapter 29

JEAN WAS on the porch outside when I drove up to the house. She gave me a nervous look as I got out and walked up the stairs.

"What's going on?" I asked anxiously. "Did something happen?"

She pulled me closer, then pointed across the street. "That car."

"What about it?"

"Someone is sitting inside it, and they've been there all day. I have a feeling this person is watching us, watching this house."

I stared at the gray Buick, scrutinizing it. I had seen it parked there in the morning when I left for work. I hadn't noticed that someone was sitting inside of it, but I did now.

"I didn't say anything to Josie. I didn't want to scare

her. That's why I thought I'd wait for you out here, so I could tell you before you went in."

Jean's blue eyes looked up at me. I felt like hugging her close to me. I didn't like seeing her in distress like this.

"Go inside," I said. "I'll deal with it."

She nodded, still looking deep into my eyes. I stared at her lips, remembering the kiss we had shared a little over a month ago. I could still feel it, and often it was the last thing I would think about before falling asleep at night. I couldn't forget about it. It was impossible.

"Okay," she said, then pulled away and walked back inside. I watched her go, and as the screened door slammed shut, I felt for my gun in my holster and kept my hand on the grip as I walked down the stairs with my eyes focused on the grey Buick. I walked quickly toward it, hoping to get to it before it could take off. Using my long legs to take big steps, I rushed toward it, and the driver didn't see me until I was almost there. He started the engine, then drove out of the parking spot.

"HEY!" I yelled and tried to step out in front of it to stop it. But the driver didn't intend to stop. He stepped on the accelerator and rushed toward me, forcing me to jump to the side of the road in order not to be hit.

I rolled in the grass, then lifted my head just in time to see the license plate and memorize it. I got to my feet and brushed off the grass, then hurried back to the house and slammed the door shut behind me, locking it carefully. I took a few breaths to calm myself. I didn't want Josie to notice that anything was wrong.

"Dad!" Josie yelled as she saw me. She hugged me, and suddenly a sweet aroma filled my nostrils.

"I've made lamb for dinner," Josie said. "Well, not completely by myself. Jean helped me."

"It smells heavenly," I said and kissed her forehead. I stared at Jean, who was checking on the meat in the oven. Lamb was one of my favorite meals, and Jean knew this. Seeing her in my kitchen cooking again made my heart overflow with happiness. I had missed her terribly over the past month. She used to take such good care of all of us, and I guess I hadn't appreciated her enough.

"Dinner will be ready in half an hour," Jean chirped. "I called your dad, and he'll be over shortly. He just got back."

I smiled happily. *Just like old times*, I thought, then felt guilty. I couldn't do this to myself. I couldn't romanticize the time before Camille woke up.

"I'm sorry I was late today," I said as I put the keys down and opened my laptop. "It wasn't my intention to ruin your entire day off."

Jean smiled. I hadn't seen that smile in quite a while, and even though I didn't want it to, it filled me with warmth.

"It's okay," she said. "I actually enjoyed myself. It feels good to be here again. Josie and I had some catching up to do."

I looked into her eyes, feeling all kinds of sadness. Why did I feel like this when looking at her? Why did I have all these emotions that I didn't have when looking at Camille? Was my dad right? He was the one who told me he believed I loved Jean more than Camille, even before Camille overdosed.

He couldn't be right, could he?

I shook my head and looked down at my computer. It didn't matter. There wasn't anything I could do about it now anyway. I was married, and my wife was sick. She needed me more than ever.

Chapter 30

WHEN SAVANNAH WOKE UP, she was lying on the floor. Her face felt sore, and her lips tasted like blood when she licked them. She felt drowsy and had a hard time opening her eyes. It was so hot; she was sweating like crazy. What was that awful smell? She tried to recall what had happened before she ended up there.

She remembered playing the violin. She remembered it getting dark and that she had decided to go to bed. Then she remembered there was a noise and then there was something else. A man, yes, that was it. A man had entered her house and was standing by the back door. Then what had happened?

"Who are you? What are you doing here?" she had asked.

The man had stepped into the light, pulling down the hood on his raincoat. That was when she had stopped breathing. Recognizing the eyes staring at her, she knew he had come for her. He had finally found her.

"I never told anyone," she said. "I kept it to myself."

But the man didn't seem to care. He rushed toward her, and as she saw that, she went for the front door. She turned around and made a run for it, but the man was faster. He grabbed her by the collar and pulled her back, then put his arm around her neck and dragged her backward.

Savannah had screamed, but he was too strong. He had punched her, then put his hands around her neck, holding tight till she had fainted.

Why am I not dead?

She asked herself this as she took a couple of breaths, trying to get back to reality. Her eyelids still felt heavy and hard to lift, so she focused on her hands, trying to move them. They weren't strapped down. The same went for her legs, and she could move them with ease. But the stench was getting worse, and it was getting harder to breathe.

What's going on here?

She finally managed to lift her eyelids and look. But all she could see was deep darkness.

Savannah sat up and tried to look around, trying to figure out where she was. She reached out her hand, and it hit something, and she felt it, then used it to lean on, to get to her feet. She recognized her bed, and leaned against it, then felt her way to the nightstand with the lamp, found the button, and turned it on. Except nothing happened. There was no light. She flipped the button again and again, but nothing happened. She then felt her way past the dresser to the door, where she flipped the switch on the wall next to it.

Still nothing.

Did the power go out?

There was like a rumbling noise coming from outside the room. Savannah walked to the window, then grabbed the thick velvet curtains that had been closed to shut out all light. As she pulled them aside, she suddenly saw light, and lots of it, in the shape of flames licking the side of the house.

Startled, Savannah pulled back with a scream.

Oh, dear God, it's a fire. Someone set fire to my house!

She backed up to get away from the window, then ran for the door. She grabbed the handle, but the door was locked.

Who locked the door? I can't get out!

Savannah pulled it, again and again, shaking the door, but it wouldn't budge. A huge pop startled her as the windows shattered, and the fire soon grabbed the curtains inside and spread to the bed, moving faster than seemed possible. Savannah screamed at the top of her lungs, then shook the door handle again and again, then started kicking the door till it finally broke open.

Thinking she had found a way out, Savannah crawled through the opening she had made and into the hallway when she realized it too was surrounded by flames on all sides.

She was trapped.

Chapter 31

AT DINNER, Camille sat in her wheelchair next to me, so I could feed her to make sure she got enough to eat. She seemed very insistent on trying on her own, so I let her eat by herself, at least till she gave up and let me take over.

After dinner, Josie, my dad, and I cleaned up while Jean took Camille to her room and put her back in bed. I told Jean she didn't have to do that, but she wanted to, she said. She loved Camille and enjoyed taking care of her again. Camille got exhausted quickly these days, but at least she was present now. It was an improvement, and hopefully to her life as well, even though there still was so much she wasn't capable of doing.

"At some point, you have to forgive her," my dad said.

Josie asked if she had helped enough by now and

would be allowed to go back upstairs. I nodded and let her leave. My dad handed me a plate, and I put it in the dishwasher. I turned to look at him once I was sure Josie was completely out of sight and wouldn't be able to hear us.

"What do you mean?"

"Camille," he said. "You're angry with her for doing drugs again and for causing this overdose, but at some point, you have to let it go, son. It'll only eat you up and come between you two."

"I've already forgiven her," I said.

"Have you now?"

I gave him another look. My dad, the former pastor, always had a way of seeing straight through me to a point where it annoyed me.

I smiled. "It's a work in progress."

"It always is," he said. "It's rarely something that happens instantly. It takes time, and sometimes it's a process that lasts an entire lifetime. But letting go of that resentment and anger toward her is vital if you want to move on."

"I know," I said, sounding like an annoyed teenager. "I just…it's still hard for me to understand why she would do it, why she would hurt us all like this."

"Pray about it," he said and handed me the last dish. I placed it in the dishwasher, then turned it on. My dad and I each grabbed a glass of iced tea and sat in the living room. I poured some in a glass for Jean and gave it to her as she came out to join us. My dad turned on the TV and watched the news, while Jean and I sat in silence for a few minutes.

"So, did you figure out who was in that car?" she asked, using a low voice. "Did you see him?"

"No, he drove off. I didn't even get a look at his face. But I did get the license plate and called it in and had them run it in the system before we ate dinner."

"Did you get a name?"

I nodded.

"So, who is it, anyone we know?"

I nodded again. "You won't believe it; I hardly did myself. It doesn't seem to make much sense. I've been pondering about it all night."

"Try me."

I leaned forward.

"David Smith."

She wrinkled her forehead. "As in the same David Smith, who is the…"

"The father of Emilia García, yes, the girl who gave Josie her heart."

Jean leaned back and took a sip from her glass of iced tea, a puzzled look on her face. "He was here? Keeping an eye on us? But…why?"

I shrugged. "Beats me. But he sure was in a hurry to get away when I approached him. I had to jump for my life so he wouldn't hit me. Scraped my arm."

"Do you want me to take a look at it?" Jean asked.

I chuckled. "I think I'll survive."

"Why do you think he was there all day? It is strange, don't you think?"

I sighed. "I don't know. There's a lot I can't seem to figure out right now. But I intend to dig deeper into it. Something is very wrong in this town, and I don't like it one bit."

Chapter 32

WHEN MY DAD LEFT, I told Josie to get ready for bed and walked Jean home. She lived right next door, but with what she had seen earlier in the day, with Emilia's dad watching us, I didn't like for her to be out on her own. I felt uneasy at the thought of him lurking out there. I was extremely grateful for what he had done, giving my daughter a new heart, and I still wanted to thank him for it, but showing up like that, sneaking around my house? Running off when I approached him? It made me very uncomfortable. I couldn't figure out why a man like him would do that. Why didn't he just come to our door if he had something he wanted to talk to us about?

Why did he rush off in such a hurry?

But if I was completely honest, it wasn't just that. I had another reason that I wanted to walk her home. I had enjoyed her company this whole evening, and frankly, I didn't want it to end.

"So…" she said as we walked up her stairs and stopped by her door. The old porch swing was moving in the wind, the chains squeaking. There was a nice breeze tonight, and it felt good on my skin.

"This is me."

"Thank you," I said with a deep sigh. "For everything. For helping out today with Josie and Camille, for cooking, for just being there and for…well… being who you are."

That made her chuckle. "Wow. That was a lot."

"I just…I don't know how to thank you enough. I know the past month has been…well, it's been terrible, to be honest. I missed you, and I know it's selfish and I…I want to make sure you understand that you don't have to hang around us if it makes you uncomfortable. I don't want to force you to come over if it's too unbearable; I hope you know this."

She placed a hand on my arm. "I know, Harry. No one is forcing me. I do it because I enjoy it. You never meant for any of this to happen. It's not your fault. None of this is. It's just…bad timing."

I nodded, pressing back tears. I looked into her eyes, feeling my emotions stir again. She smiled, her sweet eyes narrowing, creating small lines in the sides. For a second, I thought I'd kiss her, and leaned in slightly, but then pulled back.

"Maybe this isn't such a good idea," she said, and let go of my arm. "Us hanging out too much."

I nodded. She was right. What we were doing was dangerous. The more time we spent together, the more I was falling for her. But being without her this past month had made me miserable. I didn't want to go back to that.

"I'm sorry," I said. "I am so, so sorry…for everything."

She chuckled, but it didn't sound happy. She then lifted herself onto her tippy toes and placed a kiss on my cheek. I closed my eyes as her lips met my stubble, genuinely wishing it could have been on the lips.

"Good night, Harry Handsome," she whispered, her eyes closed, leaning in against me. I grabbed her wrists and took in a deep breath, smelled her, trying to take as much of her back with me as I could.

She sighed. I sighed. I could feel her warm breath against my skin. I wanted to stay like this forever. I wanted to hold her in my arms forever.

"I should go," she whispered, but she didn't pull away, and I didn't let go of her. Neither of us dared to move because, in doing so, we'd ruin the moment; we'd rip our lives apart yet again.

"I'm gonna go now," she said, finally pulling away from me. It felt like someone pulled away the very ground I stood on. I took a deep breath and looked at her again when out of the corner of my eye, I spotted someone coming down the street. A guy walking his dog. He gave us one look, then said:

"Did you guys see the fire? It looks like it's only a couple of blocks down. It looks big."

I turned around, walked down the stairs, then looked behind Jean's house where the man was pointing. And there it was. What looked like a few streets behind ours, a thick pillar of smoke reached the sky.

"Oh, dear Lord," Jean said. "I hope no one is hurt."

"I'm gonna go check it out," I said, grabbing my phone and calling nine-one-one.

"I'll go with you," Jean said and followed me into the street.

Chapter 33

FLAMES WERE LICKING the windows of the house. A window popped as we approached it, sounding like gunfire. The thick smoke was hanging deep from the ceiling, emerging through doorways and the vents. The heat greeting us was immense, like a brick wall, the air thick with toxic components from the burning synthetic materials like furniture and paint inside the house.

A couple of neighbors were outside in their front yards, looking at it, and in the distance, I could hear sirens. I had talked to dispatch, and now the firetrucks were approaching.

"Do you think whoever lives there was home when the fire started?" Jean asked.

"I hope not," I said. "With a fire like this, you'd have barely two or three minutes to get out."

As we stood there, staring at the flames, listening to the sound of them devouring the old house, we heard a sound. One so terrifying, it made my heart stop.

"Did you hear that?" I asked.

Jean gave me a look of distress.

"Yes. It sounds like…knocking."

"Someone's in there," I said. "Hammering on a door somewhere."

I looked around me, realizing the firetrucks were still at least a minute out. If this person, whoever it was, was trapped inside, there wasn't time to waste. A minute could mean the difference between life and death.

"I'm going in," I said.

"Harry, no," Jean said. "You'll only get yourself killed; the smoke alone is poisonous. You know better than this. Harry, are you listening?"

I wasn't. I had already left her and was rushing up toward the house. Thick smoke emerged from all the passageways behind the front door. The door handle had to be too hot to touch, so instead, I kicked the wood again and again. It broke into pieces, and thick warm smoke hit my face. I turned away but was still blinded by it. I coughed as the heat forced me to my hands and knees.

"Hello? Is someone in here? Hallo?" I yelled.

I crawled forward into the house, staying close to

the walls. I had been through training programs for situations like this when I was just a young police officer in the force, but that was years ago now. Yet I remembered the important stuff, like staying low, and as I was inside, I found an umbrella in the hallway, grabbed it, and used it to sweep the floors since I couldn't rely on my eyes. They were burning badly, and I kept them shut most of the time while searching the surroundings.

Then the umbrella hit something.

There was something about the sound a human body made when being hit with an object. It was one you'd recognize anywhere. I knew I would, and at this moment, I did.

I reached out my hands and felt to be certain. My fingers touched clothing. The feeling was sickening. There was no mistake; this was a person, a body. The question was whether this person was still alive.

I grabbed ahold of the body and pulled it up on my back, then began to carry it out through the thick smoke. The body was heavy, a lot heavier than you'd think. I grabbed the arms to hold it steady, but the burned skin slipped off, and I couldn't hold on properly. I crawled forward toward the door with the body on my back, crying because my eyes burned so badly, but also because of all the emotions in this instant, not knowing if this person was dead or alive.

Once I reached the porch, I fell forward onto the wood and heard voices around me. People were yelling something that I couldn't understand. Soon, black boots and yellow uniforms had surrounded me, and the weight was lifted off my back while other hands then grabbed me and lifted me as well. The last thing I saw was the ground disappearing right before I passed out.

Chapter 34

JEAN WENT with Harry in the ambulance. Her heart was throbbing in her chest as she watched him on the stretcher. He was breathing, yes, but he was completely out. Jean had seen many patients in her life as a nurse come in after a fire, then die shortly afterward. Usually, it was from inhaling carbon monoxide or other poisonous gases from burning synthetic materials on furniture or having the insides of their breathing passages burned. Harry had been inside of that burning house for way too long, without being equipped for it. It wasn't just dangerous; it was stupid and so typical of Harry.

Risking his life for some complete stranger.

It made her so angry that he'd do that. But she couldn't really be mad at him, could she? How could she be mad at a hero?

As they arrived at the hospital, Jean ran inside with them. It was strange to be on the other side in a situation like this, seeing her colleagues come running out, grabbing the stretcher, and rushing off with him. The ambulance with the woman Harry pulled out had arrived shortly before them, and she knew they were already fighting to save her life. She had heard the paramedics yell that she was still alive right before she was rushed into the ambulance. The question was for how long. Jean had seen the damage the fire had done to her body. She had been severely burned on most of her body, and Jean knew her chances were slim, very slim.

Jean was shown inside by her colleague, Tina, into the waiting room. It was so eerily silent in there, more than what Jean could bear. Time seemed to stand completely still. She stared at her phone while tapping her leg, then called Harry's dad. He didn't pick up. She tried again, but it went straight to voicemail. She knew he had a landline, but she didn't have that number. Jean sighed, then tried again before giving up. She knew Harry's dad, old Pastor Bernard, liked to go to bed early, and once he did, there was no waking him. Jean stared at the phone, then found Josie's number and was about to call her when she stopped herself. How could she explain this to the girl? They had been through so much lately, and she was not supposed to get too agitated with her new heart and all.

I need to know he's all right first. I need to have something to tell her.

Jean rubbed her forehead, then walked into the hallway, looking for anyone she could talk to. A nurse or a doctor, someone who could tell her if Harry was okay or not. It felt like she had been in that waiting room forever.

Jean walked down the hallway. She spotted one of her colleagues, then called out her name, but she continued and ran into the operating room. She wondered if Harry was there. Had he suffered burns?

The doors suddenly slammed open, and Jean stepped aside. They rushed someone out of the room, and Jean gasped when she realized it was the woman Harry had helped out of the house. As they rushed her out and down the hallway, Jean locked eyes with her, and she saw such deep terror in them, her heart almost stopped. The woman was breathing in puffs; her skin so burned it was falling off in flakes. It was a gruesome sight. It was hard to see that she was even human behind the disfigured skin.

As her eyes met Jean's, it was like she tried to get Jean's attention. Jean held her breath and stared at her as she passed, while the woman's mouth moved. As Jean looked at her, she realized the woman was speaking, that her mouth was shaping two words.

Two words that would stay with Jean for the rest of her life.

The woman had barely let them leave her lipless mouth when her EKG monitor flatlined, and all the alarms sounded.

Chapter 35

"STOP FUSSING OVER ME; I am perfectly fine."

I growled at the nurse. She had just told me they wanted me to stay at the hospital for a few hours. I had told her a million times that I had to get home to my daughter and that I was all right.

"So, this is where you're hiding."

"Jean," I said, smiling as I saw her gentle eyes lingering on me from the doorway. "Tell her I'm fine; will you?"

She gave me a look, lifting her eyebrows.

"Are you?"

"Yes!" I groaned. "I'm perfectly fine. You can read the darn report yourself. It'll tell you I'm great and ready to go. No severe burns, only some mild ones to my leg, but it's nothing. And I have no signs of smoke inhalation. They took an x-ray of my chest to see if there was damage to my lungs; they checked my oxygen levels and the levels of carbon monoxide in my blood. The doctor said it's all good."

Jean sighed. I could tell she wasn't sure she believed me. She always thought I exaggerated just how fine I was. She grabbed my phone from the table next to me.

"Here. You need to call your daughter and tell her where you are and don't forget to mention how you got yourself into this trouble."

"All right," I said and grabbed it, "but then can you do something for me?"

Jean rolled her eyes with a sigh, then smiled as I pleaded with my hands clasped together.

"There's always something with you, isn't there? Like what, might I ask?"

"Find out how she's doing."

"Who."

"The girl I pulled from the house."

"Oh, Harry…" Jean's face went blank. I sank back in the bed, leaning against the pillow at my back.

"Oh. Are you su…"?

Jean shook her head, her eyes overwhelmed with despair. "I am sorry. She died just now in the hallway. They were transferring her to the Burn Center. They resuscitated her, but her heart failed. And that was it. She's gone."

Tears welled up in my eyes. I couldn't believe this. It had all been in vain? I had risked my life…for this?

Only for her to die in the hospital? The thought was unbearable, cruel.

"What…what was her name?" I asked.

"Savannah Hart."

"Savannah Hart," I repeated pensively. I wanted to remember her.

"But there is something else," Jean said as the nurse left us. She closed the curtain around me so no one could see us. She sat on the edge of the bed.

"What?"

"She said something to me right before she died."

I made a face. What was she talking about?

"You were there? When she died? I don't get it."

"I saw her when she was being transported down the hallway. Our eyes locked, and then she mouthed two words to me that I can't forget. Her eyes were so insistent; it still gives me goosebumps to think about it. It was like she knew she was going to die, and it was important for her to get this message across to someone before she went. I can't explain it; I just knew it was important."

"And what did she say? What were those two words?"

Jean leaned over and whispered in my ear. As she spoke, my eyes grew wider, and my heart started to pound loudly. I could barely believe her. With two small words, shaping a name, some of the pieces in my puzzle suddenly fell into place. Not all of them, but enough for me to understand that this woman wasn't in an accident. She was killed by the same murderer that had killed Major Wolfe, and if Josie's heart told the truth, the same person who had also murdered Emilia and Jennifer García.

Chapter 36

"TIMOTHY WILSON."

I kept repeating the name over and over again in the Uber on my way home. Jean was sitting next to me, yawning. I couldn't blame her. I was exhausted too. I had called and spoken to Josie, then told her not to worry and just go to bed, that I'd be home soon. I just hoped she had been able to fall asleep. She needed all the rest she could get.

"I remembered you told me that was the name on the guy's grave," Jean said, "the one where you found your old boss. That's why it startled me so much. Do you have any idea why she'd say that name?"

I shook my head. "Not really, other than she must have known Major Wolfe was buried there. Just like Emilia knew."

"Do you think she might have seen who killed him

and buried him?" Jean said as the driver drove up in front of my house. I thanked him for the ride, and we both got out.

"That is exactly what I think. You have a very sharp mind, Miss Wilcox," I said, teasing her. "We could use someone like you on the force one day."

She scoffed. "I'll just end up having to patch you all up when some tough guy roughs you up. I'd end up babysitting all of you."

I exhaled as the Uber disappeared down the road.

"Thank you…again," I said. "For staying with me tonight when I was in the hospital. That means a lot."

She smiled, "Ah, don't go all soft on me, Hunter. You know I'll always be there for you. Besides, I had to make sure you were all right and that you didn't drive the nurses crazy. Now, remember, if you have any signs…"

"I know, I know. Cough, shortness of breath, headache, any changes in my skin…if it turns blue or pale due to lack of oxygen, if I feel confused, if I faint, if I experience chest pain…did I leave anything out?"

"Maybe just vomiting blood; that's something to look out for too."

"Isn't it always?" I asked with a grin.

"This is no joke, Harry Hunter. You listen to me. You come knocking on my door if you have any of those symptoms, okay?" she said. "Or call nine-one-one right away. It's up to you. But don't ignore it; you hear me?"

I nodded. "Yes, ma'am. Loud and clear. Now, goodnight."

Jean sighed. Her shoulders came down slightly. It had been a tough night for her too. I hated that I made her worry.

"Good night, Harry. Take care."

I sent her one last look as she walked up to her porch and I to mine. I smiled as I saw that she looked at me too, right before we both walked inside. I still felt like I could smell the darn smoke everywhere, and my throat was scratchy. I went to get a glass of water in the kitchen first, to bring with me up to bed.

I had barely turned on the light in the kitchen when I heard a loud bump coming from upstairs. When I looked out in the street, I saw the gray Buick parked a couple of houses down under a streetlight.

What in the…?

Wasting no more time, I hurried into the hallway and grabbed my gun from the safety box in the closet, using my fingerprints to open it. With the gun held out in front of me, I walked as quietly as possible up the stairs.

Chapter 37

THE GUN WAS steady in my hand as I was reminding myself to be cautious not to overreact. After all, the bumping sounds could easily have been Josie going to the bathroom, or maybe she hadn't gone to bed at all after we spoke. But the sight of the Buick in the street made me suspect otherwise, and I wasn't taking any chances.

I reached the top of the stairs when I saw a shadow move across the hallway…the shadow of a person who looked nothing like Josie.

"Stop right there," I said.

He did as I told him.

"Hands where I can see them, behind your head."

The person obeyed. Hands were placed behind the neck.

"Now, turn around."

As I suspected, I was looking at David Smith. He was shaking heavily.

"What are you doing in my home?" I asked and stepped forward, holding the gun out. I felt such anger swell up inside of me and had to keep my cool so it wouldn't run away with me. It was one thing that he was watching us from the street, but having him break into my house where my daughter was sleeping all alone was something completely different.

"Answer me! What are you doing here? Did you hurt my daughter?"

He shook his head. "N-no."

"What's going on?"

Josie came out through her door and looked at us.

"Are you okay?" I asked. "Did he touch you?"

Josie shook her head. "No. I didn't…who is he, and why is he here…Dad?"

"She was sleeping," David said, stuttering. "I was just…watching her."

"You were watching her sleep?" I asked. "Why?"

David sank to his knees, crying. "Don't you understand? She's all I have left of her. She's all I have left of Emilia. She has her heart…pounding in her chest, my daughter's heart."

"What?" Josie asked. "He's her dad?"

"Is that why you've been watching us?" I asked.

He nodded, sobbing. "Yes. That and because I needed to protect her."

"What do you mean protect her?" I asked, confused.

David pressed back tears and swallowed before he spoke. "Someone wants her dead."

"Someone wants my Josie dead?" I asked. "Who?"

"I don't know," David said, crying.

I stepped forward and placed the gun to his head, then yelled:

"WHO?"

David was trembling beneath the gun. "I don't know him. I don't know his name or who he is, but I know he works at the harbor. I've done a couple of gigs for him, you know…transport. Stuff like that, illegal transport. He imports appliances, fridges, freezers, washer and dryers, stuff like that under the radar. Avoiding taxes and stuff like that. I don't know much about it except I sometimes drive one of their trucks. That's all. I owe money, a lot of it, and they pay me well. Better than any other driving job. As long as I don't ask any questions. Anyway, I heard him talking to someone about it a few days ago, about the girl, the daughter of a detective and how the heart, my Emilia's heart, had led them to find the body of some guy that they wanted to stay buried. I knew it could only be Josie they were talking about. They talked about cutting that heart out of the girl, getting rid of her. I thought I could protect her. As I told you, she's all I have left of my girl, my sweet daughter."

"Why didn't you just come to talk to me? You could've warned me instead of hanging out in the street like that," I said, still angry, but easing up slightly.

"I panicked. I wanted to see Josie, to see her with my daughter's heart, and then when you came out to the car, I freaked out. I panicked, and then I thought you wouldn't talk to me after I almost ran you over."

"Well, you're right about that. No one listens to someone creeping around like some snake. I'm not even sure I believe half of what you're saying right now."

Josie came up behind me. "Dad, listen to the man. Look at him. He doesn't look like much of a threat, does he? Don't forget what he did for me."

"He broke into our home, Josie. This is our sacred place. Here, I expect you to be safe. He violated that."

She placed a hand on the gun and lowered it while looking into my eyes. I eased up. No one could soften me up like Josie.

"Who were these men?" I asked David. "The ones you heard talk about Josie?"

He shook his head. "I don't know their names."

I lifted the gun again. "You're gonna help me catch them. But not till we've gotten Josie to a safe place."

Chapter 38

"WHAT'S THIS?"

Al stared at Josie, her eyes squinting. She was fully dressed, even though it was three a.m.

"It's my daughter. Josie, this is Al; Al, meet Josie. Get used to one another. She's going to stay here for a little while."

"She's what?"

Al stared at me, but I pushed past her inside and walked to a couch, then told Josie to lie down on it.

"Do you have a blanket? Josie needs rest. Her heart, you know."

Al stared at me, her mouth still half open. She slammed the door shut behind us and put the many safety locks back on.

"Now, wait a second, I have never…I'm not…children and I are not a mix."

"Blanket, please," I said, ignoring her.

Al walked to her closet, grabbed a blanket, then handed it to me. I used it to cover Josie, then kissed her, and told her to sleep. It didn't take a second before her eyes were closed and she was breathing heavily. She needed it.

"Are you even listening to me?" Al said.

I pulled her to the other end of the room, so our talking wouldn't wake Josie. "Listen, I get it. You don't like children. But Josie is fourteen. She's not a child. Christ, she's twice your size, if you haven't noticed."

"A lot of children are taller than me; that doesn't mean they don't cause trouble or make a mess," she snorted. "I'm not the motherly type."

I sighed and ran a hand through my hair. "I need this."

She gave me a look.

"Remember your sister and how I found the guy who killed her?"

Al groaned loudly. "Oh, you're gonna pull that one on me, huh?"

"You said a lifetime of help."

"I meant on computers. Hacking stuff. Not babysitting."

"She's in danger," I said. "They want to kill her. I can't go into too many details, but she helped find a body that was supposed to stay hidden. You're the only one I trust right now. No one knows this place even exists. It's a freaking fortress."

Al exhaled and fiddled with a dreadlock. "All right, I guess. But I'm not cooking or anything like that."

"You don't have to," I said and handed her a one-hundred-dollar bill. "Buy a pizza. Buy several since Josie eats a lot. She's still growing."

"I wouldn't think it was possible for her to get any taller, but I'll take your word for it," she said and took the bill.

"Just don't let her leave the apartment, okay? I need her to stay hidden," I said, about to walk to the door.

"I haven't left this place in years, at least not in full daylight," Al said. "I think I can manage. But, hey, be safe out there, will ya?"

I chuckled. "And you say you're not the motherly type. That right there was some pretty deep motherly stuff."

"Get out of here," Al said. "Before I kick you out."

"Oh, before I forget," I said and stopped myself halfway to the door. "There is one more thing I need you to do for me, something I know you're very good at."

Al rolled her eyes at me. "You're the gift that just keeps on giving, aren't you? Okay, Hunter. Spit it out. What is it?"

Chapter 39

I KNOCKED ON THE DOOR, then poked my head inside. It was the next morning after only a few hours of restless sleep. I had a pounding headache but ignored it, knowing Jean would kill me if she knew.

"You got a minute?"

Fowler was on the phone when he saw me. He nodded and signaled for me to give him a minute while he finished his conversation. Then he hung up.

"Hunter." He looked at his watch. "This early? Something must be up."

I sat down in a chair across from him.

"I know that look," he said and leaned back in his leather chair, folding his hands in front of him. "It usually means trouble."

"It's the Wolfe murder," I said. "You know how Josie helped find where he was buried, right?"

Fowler chuckled. "Allegedly because she dreamt it, yes, how could I forget? Has she had any other dreams recently?"

"None that she has told me about, but I have reason to believe she's in danger."

"Really?"

"Yes, whoever killed Wolfe is trying to get to her."

He got a serious look on his face. I thought about David and how he was doing back at the house where I had cuffed him and put him in the pantry, then closed the door. Camille was the only one in the house, and she would be sleeping most of the day. I reminded myself to start looking for a nurse for her. Jean was wonderful, but it wasn't healthy for any of us that she came over so often. It broke my heart to think this way, but it was necessary.

"And you're certain about this?" Fowler asked.

"I'm not making this up, if that's what you're suggesting," I said. "I have this from a reliable source."

He nodded. "Okay. Have you gotten her somewhere safe?"

I nodded. "She's staying with Al."

Fowler smiled. "I remember her. You still see each other?"

"Occasionally," I said.

Fowler had been my partner back when we had been on Al's sister's case. It was around the time he received news of his promotion, and I had ended up solving it alone while he moved up the ranks instead.

"Okay," he said. "And what do you need my help for, then?"

"I need to re-open the García case. I think they were killed because the girl knew who killed Wolfe. These two cases are deeply connected, and I want the means to solve them. I also think it's connected to the death of Savannah Hart, who died in a fire last night. I believe she was murdered too."

He wrinkled his forehead. "Do you have any evidence to back up this claim? It takes hard evidence to reopen a case; you know that."

"I'll have it hopefully by the end of the week. I have a hunch I will."

Fowler nodded. "Okay, then. You've always had good hunches. If you can provide proof enough, then the case is all yours, but it won't make you popular with your colleagues. You're basically questioning another detective's work and claiming he didn't do his job properly."

I rose to my feet, phone in my hand.

"I'm a big boy. I can take it."

Chapter 40

"DO YOU HAVE ANY SODAS?"

Josie looked at Al, the strange woman in harem pants who was sitting by her many computer screens, staring at them steadily, her fingers tapdancing across her many keyboards.

She didn't answer…maybe because she had on that big headset. Probably listening to music or speaking with someone at the other end of the world. She had been like this for the past four hours, ever since Josie woke up, and she was beginning to get bored. Her dad had taken her phone, so she couldn't be traced, and she didn't have her computer or her sketchbook with her either. There was nothing to do. Plus, she was starving. Al had been awake when she woke up, and she wondered if she had slept at all. The constant tapping on her keyboard was annoying, and she didn't like the way her eyes didn't look away from the screen…not even once. It was like she was hypnotized by that blue light like her very soul was sucked into the screen in front of her and couldn't let go. Josie had asked for food, for cereal or even some bread, but Al hadn't answered her.

Now, Josie rose to her feet and walked to the kitchen, then looked in the fridge. There was nothing much in there. Just some pomegranate, some kind of weird looking juice, and a pineapple. Was that all this woman ate?

No wonder she was the size of an ant.

Josie filled a glass of water from the fridge, then drank it, but it didn't help anything. She felt weak because she hadn't eaten for so long. It wasn't good for her heart to be fasting. She wondered if she should go and ask Al about food, like go up to her and get in her face to get her attention. Maybe pull off the headset.

Nah, she's busy and doesn't have time to take care of you. You heard her last night. She didn't want to babysit. She doesn't like children.

Josie didn't like to impose or be in the way. She wasn't one to demand much of people around her, and especially not if she sensed they didn't like her or want her around. More often than not, she was certain that if she didn't do things right or behave well enough, she'd lose people—like her dad would get mad at her and leave her. It was a real fear she'd had ever since her mother overdosed. She'd always felt it was her fault, that it was something she'd said or done to upset her enough to make her start doing drugs again. She often feared she was the one who had driven her mother to do the drugs again somehow, and now she was terrified of doing the same thing to her father. That's why she hadn't told him about how she felt that something was wrong with her heart before all of this happened. Before she passed out, she'd feel weak from time to time, especially when doing sports; she could get very dizzy. But she didn't dare to tell him. She didn't like for him to worry about her. Worry wasn't good for anyone. It made people sick. She knew that more than anyone because she worried a lot herself. She worried about her dad getting shot at work; she worried her mother would never get back to normal again. She worried that God would take them both from her, and she'd end up all alone. She worried about those things too much.

Josie felt a pinch in her heart as her stomach rumbled. She grabbed the strange juice and poured herself a glass of it, then took a deep sip. It tasted awful. She spit it all out in the sink, then washed her mouth with water. She went to the fridge, stared at the pomegranate, then decided it wasn't worth even trying. She looked at her watch.

"Could we order pizza?" she asked. "My dad said we could?"

Al was deeply into her work, and, of course, she

didn't hear. Josie sighed deeply, then walked back to the couch where she had slept. The couch was way too short, and she woke up with pain in her legs and hips.

If only she had her phone, she could call her dad and ask him to bring her food. Had he completely forgotten about her? It was one in the afternoon, and she was starving.

Josie sat down with a deep sigh, and looked at the door, willing him to come.

Bring pizza. Bring pizza!

As she sat there, staring at the door, it was like it suddenly exploded. Josie screamed as men entered the apartment, men wearing black masks and holding weapons. They pointed them at Josie and hit Al with a stick on the back of her head, so she passed out.

Next, a man entered, a man in a black suit, walking toward her with a grin on his face, his haunting steel-gray eyes glaring down at her.

"Hello, Josie," he said. "I think it's time you and I met properly, don't you think?"

Chapter 41

I RAN my bike across town, zigzagging through traffic, making sure that if anyone followed me, I'd lose them easily. I made a quick stop at one of my favorite pizza places on the beach. I asked them to make me a large pizza with ham and cheese, then drove up the small alley toward Al's building. I grabbed the pizza, ran up the back entrance and up the stairs, whistling. I had a good feeling about this case. I was going to solve it with the help of David Smith, who was still cuffed to a pipe in my pantry. I was going to him next, making sure he didn't starve to death in my house. I knew it wasn't very nice of me to cuff him like that, but I had to make sure he didn't leave. I needed his help to catch this killer. Without him, I was lost. He knew when the next delivery was due down at the harbor, and that was when they'd be there again, those men that had spoken about Josie and cutting her heart out. He had told me he was hired to do the next job tomorrow night. I just hoped Al would find me some evidence I could use against them. If all went well, I could have a team with me at the harbor and nail them once their delivery came in. But the illegal import of appliances wasn't exactly enough for me. I needed them to go down for the murder of Wolfe, and hopefully, Savannah Hart, along with Emilia and Jennifer García as well. I just didn't have all the pieces put together yet, and I hoped Al would provide me with that.

Knowing her, she'd been at it all day and had completely forgotten to feed my daughter. That was why I brought pizza. I felt compelled to, somehow. Maybe it was just my common sense.

I ran up the first flight of stairs, pizza balancing on my hand, the intense smell of it in my nostrils, making me realize I was actually starving. It wasn't exactly heart-healthy food for my daughter, but it was the best I could do right now. It was better than her not eating.

As I reached the top of the stairs, my heart suddenly dropped. The door to Al's apartment was gone. I could barely breathe when I saw it. Al never left it open. She locked it with at least five locks. As I approached it, I realized the door was on the floor inside the apartment, splintered to pieces.

Inside, I saw Al lying on the floor, blood smeared in her hair.

I threw the pizza down and ran to her.

"Al!"

She groaned something and tried to lift her head but couldn't.

"Careful," I said. "You've gotten a blow to your head. Come, let me help."

I helped her back up into her chair, where she sat for a few seconds, staring at me like she couldn't focus properly…like she had to figure out who I was. I grabbed her some water, and she drank.

"Josie," I said nervously. "Where is she?"

Al seemed to have to think it over for a few seconds. "I was…working on that thing you asked me to and didn't…I wasn't looking. I wasn't paying attention. Suddenly, there was movement; someone approached me faster than I could react, and I felt something hit the back of my head. I am sorry, Hunter. I completely blacked out."

"Who was it? Who took her?" I asked, my voice shaking in despair. "Who took my Josie?"

"I didn't get a look at them, but I have cameras. The entire place is covered."

Wincing in pain, she leaned over her computer, then clicked a few times with the mouse and wrote a passcode to something. A picture showed up on the screen, a picture of the door. The door was then kicked in, and two men in black masks and clothing entered, pointing big guns at Josie. Then, a man entered, wearing a suit. With fists clenched and heart throbbing, I watched him talk to Josie. Then the men grabbed her and carried her out, kicking and screaming. Al stopped the video right before the man in the black suit turned around and was about to leave.

"There you go," she said. "That's your guy."

"I can't believe it," I said and rubbed my hair. I stared at the face, my nostrils flaring and blood boiling.

"There's more," she said, wincing again in pain. "I found this for you. It had been deleted from Savannah Hart's cloud on the night she died, but I managed to recreate it. Here you go. This is what this guy is so eager to cover up. This is why both Savannah Hart and Emilia García had to die."

Al pressed play, and I watched the shocking video for a couple of seconds, then asked her to play it again and again. Then I asked her to send the file to my phone before I left in a fire of rage. I couldn't believe I had been so stupid all along. I had been trusting the wrong people.

Chapter 42

"GOD, give me the strength to not blow his head off because I will do it if you don't stop me."

I mumbled the words as I ran up the stairs and burst inside. I threw my helmet on the couch, then grabbed my gun, and pulled it out of the holster. I grabbed the door to the pantry, then pulled it open, pointing the gun at David, who was still sitting inside on the floor, cuffed to the pipe on the wall behind him.

He gasped when he saw me. My six feet eight could be very intimidating when I wanted them to be.

"You betrayed me, why?" I asked. "How did you know where to find her? How did you know where Josie was? Because I don't remember telling you."

David stared up at me, his hands shaking. "I don't know…what are you…I've been here the whole time."

"Cut the crap," I said and walked closer with the

gun, finger steadily on the trigger. Boy, I wanted to kill him, right then and there. Just pull the trigger and get it over with. I was that angry at this point, and sick of being deceived. I had truly believed this guy, trusted that all he wanted was to protect Josie and Emilia's heart. I had believed that he was just a grieving father who wanted to be close to whatever was left of his daughter. I had even felt sorry for him.

I felt like the biggest fool on earth.

"I'm sick of your lies. I saw you," I said. "On that video that Savannah Hart made before her death. The one from the graveyard where you shot Wolfe. I saw you, and then I saw Emilia, your daughter. You were arguing, weren't you? You had asked Wolfe to meet you there, hadn't you? And then you were arguing. Emilia was there, playing. Being homeless after you left them, her mother often let her run around in parks and at the cemetery while she was passed out on pills, sleeping in the car. That evening, she had parked next to the cemetery, and Emilia was playing around when she suddenly heard voices and hid behind a tombstone. Someone was arguing, and one of the voices sounded familiar. The girl then peeked up and, seeing her father, the man she hadn't seen in a very long time, she called out to him just as the shots were fired. Terrified, she realized she had just witnessed her own dad kill someone, and she screamed. Then, she took off running.

Seeing this, you ran after her, trying to catch her.

Meanwhile, Savannah Hart was out on one of her evening jogs, as she usually was at that time of the day, when the air is cooling down after sunset. She was in her own thoughts when she heard the shots go off and found herself right outside the cemetery. She heard the scream that followed it and realized something was very much off. Thinking she was unarmed, and her only weapon was her phone, she pulled it out and started filming between the trees. She filmed the body on the ground and then turned it to film you as you ran for the girl and grabbed her just as she reached the exit. On the video, I saw how you were holding the girl's mouth, covering it, and I could hear you hushing her, telling her it was all right and just to make sure she stayed quiet. Seeing this, Savannah knew she had to do something to save the girl, so she yelled at you. Filming you and coming up toward you, she told you to *let go of the girl*. On the video, you can clearly hear her tell you that she is live streaming it, probably thinking that will make you stop, which she is right about. You let go of Emilia, and she ran off. *Run, Girl, Run,* Savannah yelled after her. But as she made it into the street, Emilia ran into someone else, a buddy of yours. He was waiting by your car, waiting for you to finish the business he asked you to do, killing Wolfe. He's a guy with steel-gray eyes, who Emilia didn't know. Savannah was filming the encounter, and the guy saw her and forgot about Emilia, who ran with all she had while the man approached Savannah, yelling at her to stop filming.

That's when the filming stopped, and I assume Savannah ran off and later made it home. But you and your buddy then decided to go after them both, didn't you? He said he'd take care of Emilia, your daughter, and you could focus on the runner, on Savannah. So you kept an eye on the area for a little while, and one day you saw her running again, then made sure you followed her home and to work, and knew all of her routines before you made your move, didn't you? You burned down the house with her inside of it after you had made sure to remove the video from her phone and computer. But the thing is, those things never really disappear."

I raised my phone and played the video clip again. I let him watch as he saw his daughter run, and right when he grabbed her, I paused it. "There you have it. Now, I've made sure that this clip is safe somewhere in cyberspace, so if anything happens to me, the clip will be the evidence. You can't outrun it."

David's eyes didn't leave the screen and the picture of his daughter. Tears sprang to his eyes.

"She was your own daughter, for crying out loud," I said with disgust. "What kind of man are you?"

"I swear to God; I never meant for this to happen," he said. "This is a nightmare. I told you I had gotten in with the wrong crowd. I was in trouble. I owed money, and this was my way out. I feared it might end up hurting my family; that's why I left them. To protect them from these people."

"Yet, that's exactly what happened anyway," I said. "You sure messed that one up."

David's eyes were spilling over with tears, and he was shaking his head like he had trouble believing it all, like the realization of what he had done hadn't sunk in until now.

"Please," he said. "Please, don't… They said they'd kill me if I didn't kill her. They were both witnesses, both girls were. They couldn't let them live to tell what they saw. These people, you don't joke around with them. I comfort myself with the fact that I didn't kill my daughter or my ex-wife."

"Yes, you did. You just let someone else do the dirty work for you. It doesn't make you innocent. You might as well save it for someone who cares. I don't have time to listen to your self-pity or excuses," I said, stopping him before he began pleading for my mercy on his damned soul because I had none left for him right now. It was out of my hands.

"You can repent in front of God, and He'll take it from there," I said. "But for now, I need you to tell me where Josie is. You take me to her right now. I *will* shoot you if you don't. This is your chance to make something right again or die here. And don't doubt I will do it. It'll be the easiest thing in the world for me. See, without my daughter, I'm nothing. If anything happens to Josie, I will lose any will to live. The way I see it, I have nothing to lose at this point."

I pressed the gun against his forehead, and he whimpered.

"All right, all right. There's a warehouse on the port. That's probably where they have taken her."

"What warehouse? There are tons of them down there."

"It has a number on the side, two-eighty-one. It's a blue building. You can easily find it."

I shook my head. "You're coming with me. You'll show me which one."

I reached over and released his cuffs, then placed them back on his wrists while keeping his hands behind his back, so he couldn't surprise me. I was done trusting this guy. I was done trusting anyone.

Chapter 43

SHE COULDN'T SEE ANYTHING. The man with the steel-gray eyes had blindfolded her and gagged her, then tied her hands behind her back and tied her legs. They had then put her inside of something like a box. She lay curled up into a ball in this compartment, and she couldn't move. Josie had never been more afraid in her life, except for the time she had come home and found her dad and mom in the living room, her mom with foam coming out of her mouth, her dad screaming for her to call nine-one-one. That was the worst day of her life. This came in as a close second.

Dad will find me. Of course, he will.

But he might not even know she was missing. Maybe he was still at work and wasn't planning on stopping by Al's apartment till tonight? Who knew where they might have taken her at that point? She didn't even know where they were going, only that she was moving, swaying along inside her bubble.

Where are they taking me?

The man with the steel-gray eyes had touched her chest before she was taken away. He had touched it gently, then placed an ear against it like he was listening to it. Then he had laughed and told her how amazing the human body was and what it was capable of.

"To think that it could tell you about me, huh?" he had asked while gently caressing her cheek. "Yes, I know your heart snitched on me. Aw, what's that face? Don't look so upset; it'll only hurt when we take it out. After that, you won't feel a thing. I promise."

The last part was said with a huge grin, and then his men had picked her up, blindfolded her, and taken her away. She had tried to scream and fight them, but it was no use.

Now, as she lay there inside her own darkness, all she could do was pray…pray like her dad had taught her to when in trouble. Pray the same way she had when her mother had overdosed. Pray the same way she had every day for three years while her mother was nothing but a vegetable. Josie had fought not to lose hope during that time, but it had been a tough fight. It was so hard to believe that a miracle could happen after all this time, and she kept fearing it wasn't going to. She had remembered her granddad's words every time doubt hit her like a freight train: "Sometimes our lives don't turn out the way we want them to. That's when we need faith to kick in. Trust that God knows what he is doing. Trust his timing."

Back then, she hadn't understood much of what it meant, but now she did. Once her mother had finally come back, it had been such a big miracle; it almost seemed impossible.

As she lay inside that small compartment she was being transported in, thinking about her mother and the miracle they had experienced helped strengthen her faith. She was afraid, yes, scared to death. But she also knew what God was capable of. And she had to trust him once again. Even though it was hard to, she had to do it. She simply had to because it was all she had.

Without faith, there was only fear.

Without hope, she was lost.

Chapter 44

"IT'S that one right over there, the blue one."

David nodded to show me which building it was since he couldn't use his hands or fingers to point. I spotted the building and then the number on the side of it. Two hundred and eighty-one. I parked my city-issued Chevrolet behind the neighboring building and got out. I walked to David's door, opened it, and helped him out as well, holding my gun into his side, making sure he understood the rules.

"No games," I whispered in his ear, pressing the gun hard into his side.

I let him lead the way as we approached a big white truck and walked past it. I looked into the back of it before we continued to make sure Josie wasn't in there or anyone who might surprise us from behind. The truck seemed to be in the process of being filled with appliances…what looked like a couple of fridges, several dryers, and at least one washing machine. It wasn't even half-filled, so I knew someone would be there soon, probably bringing in more, and hurried past it toward the blue building before we were seen.

"No, not the front," I said and stopped him as he was about to lead us to the big opening of the warehouse. I heard the sound of a forklift coming from in there; maybe there was more than one.

"There must be a side entrance or a back door or something," I said.

"Over there," he said and nodded. I turned to see a small door in the side of the building.

"Perfect," I said.

I opened it as silently as possible and pushed David in first in case there was a guard in there, but he just walked straight in, gun placed against the back of his head.

"Now, take me to him," I said.

"Are you sure?" he whispered back. "I mean, there's one of you, and he has his own army."

"I don't care," I said.

"I sure hope that God of yours is keeping an eye out on you today," he mumbled. "You're walking straight into the lion's den."

"And I won't even smell like smoke when I come out," I said, "now, show me the way."

"It's your funeral," he said, then walked forward.

He stopped at another door that I had to open for him, one that led into the big hall where the forklifts were working, grabbing the brand-new still wrapped appliances one after another, transporting them out to the truck. There was a lot of noise, and no one noticed that we entered. The first guy who did see us went for his gun immediately, and I pulled mine from David's head, pointed it at him, then fired. I hit him in the shoulder, right in the spot that I knew would make him drop the gun. And it did. The gun fell to the cement floor below, and the guy fell to his knees in pain, holding his bloody shoulder.

Now, all eyes were on us.

The forklifts stopped what they were doing, and anyone working there stared first at me and then at David. I placed the gun to the side of David's head to make sure they could all see it.

"I need to see him," I said. "Now."

Chapter 45

"WHAT'S GOING ON HERE? Why have you stopped working?"

Ferdinand came out from behind the glass window leading to the back office. He took one glance at me with his steel-gray eyes, then nodded.

"Ah, I see."

He looked at me, then at David before he stepped forward.

"Stay where you are," I said. "One step closer, and he's toast."

"What do you want, Hunter?" Ferdinand asked with a deeply annoyed sigh. "Why have you come?"

"I want my daughter back," I said. "Where is she?"

"Your daughter?" he said with a grin. "You've come here looking for your daughter? Well, she's not here. I don't have time to have young girls running around here. It would be way too dangerous, anyway."

"I know everything," I said. "I know what you two did. I have the video. The one Savannah Hart took on that night at the cemetery. I know you killed Emilia and Jennifer García. I know David killed Savannah Hart and Major Wolfe."

The grin on Ferdinand's face had faded. He still stared at me like he was contemplating what his next move should be.

"What did you do with her, Ferdinand? And don't tell me she isn't here because I know she is. I know you took her."

"Well, you're welcome to have a look around," he said. "See if you can see her anywhere."

I threw a glance around the warehouse, my heart pounding in my chest. Where could he be keeping her? A couple of his goons had their hands inside their jackets, waiting for me to make a mistake so they could pull their weapons and finish me off. They had all seen what happened to the first guy who tried and didn't dare to yet. But it would only take me letting my guard down for a split second for them to make their move.

"No? Well, then, let us get back to work, will you?" Ferdinand said. "We have a shipment that needs to be in Chicago by tomorrow night."

I stared at the appliances, all gathered up against the wall across from me. One forklift had stopped not far from me with a dryer barely lifted off the ground. I kept staring at it while so many questions piled up inside of me. There was so much I still didn't understand.

I bit my lip, then turned to look at Ferdinand.

"It's not just appliances, is it? I mean, I keep wondering what's so lucrative about importing appliances illegally. Is that worth risking your career? Risk going to jail?"

I walked to the dryer on the forklift, holding David close to me. He was my collateral. My theory was that he and Ferdinand were partners in this, and Ferdinand needed him. At least I hoped he did. I let go of David, then reached over and pulled the bubble wrap off the dryer just enough to be able to open it. I pulled the door open, then peeked inside.

The sight that met me from in there almost made me lose it. I had a lot of theories as to what they were, in fact, transporting, but I could still barely believe what I was seeing.

Chapter 46

JOSIE GASPED FOR AIR. It was getting tight where she was, and she was fighting to breathe properly. It was hot too. Unbearably hot. She was constantly sweating, and her throat was scratchy from thirst.

She hadn't moved for quite some time now and was getting anxious and restless. It was hard not to panic when you couldn't move.

Please, God, have someone find me. Lead my dad to find me. I know he'll listen to you. Don't let me down. Don't forget about me.

Josie laid still while sweat trickled down her forehead and landed on her lip. It tasted salty and made her feel even more thirsty. Josie would do anything right now for something to drink. After hours inside this place, she was beginning to feel dizzy and like she couldn't stay awake much longer. She kept dozing off and waking up again, and she knew dehydration was starting to set in. It wasn't good for her heart, and she had more than once felt a huge pinch, one that made her cry out behind the gag. And now she felt it again. A stabbing pain went through her chest, and she was certain she was running a fever too. The tiredness, the weakness, along with shortness of breath and tightness of her chest were some of the symptoms she could feel if her body was rejecting the heart, she had been told.

She was feeling all of that right now. All of it.

This was too much strain and stress on her heart. Her body couldn't cope with it anymore.

Hurry up, God. It's getting serious now. I'm running out of time. Get my dad to me, please.

A few tears rolled down her cheeks as she dozed off, then woke up again, only to realize she was still in the same darkness but feeling even more tired now. She closed her eyes again and thought of her family, of how happy they had been once, how happy she had been when she was just a child. Before everything went bad. Before her mom had…

Josie dozed off once again in the middle of a thought, no longer having the strength to fight the luring sleep calling for her.

In the distance, she thought she heard her father's voice, but she didn't know if it was just part of her dream.

A few seconds later, it didn't matter anymore.

Chapter 47

THE ANXIOUS BROWN eyes looking back at me from inside the dryer blinked a few times while deciding whether to trust me or not. They belonged to a young boy, nine, maybe ten years old.

The realization of what I had found made me cry out with distress. I pulled back and looked at Ferdinand, shaking my head in disgust.

"A…a child?"

He narrowed his eyes while looking at me. "Maybe you ought to stop now, Harry. Before you go where there is no way back."

"Oh, I think we've reached that point, don't you think?" I asked, biting back my tears. "I think we're way past that."

I turned to face the stacked appliances leaned up against the wall in front of me, on top of one another, as high as the ceiling. How many were there? One hundred? Two hundred?

Heart throbbing in my chest, I ran to the front of the stack, ripped off the bubble wrap, and opened a freezer. Another set of anxious eyes was staring back at me while the mouth gasped for air. The woman reached out her hand toward me. It seemed she was more dead than alive. I kept the lid open, then ripped the cardboard off the next one, where I found another young boy, maybe fourteen.

Who were these people?

"Where do they come from?" I asked while opening the next, frantically pulling at the wrapping, tears streaming across my cheeks. The cruelty in this seemed impossible.

"Who knows?" Ferdinand said. "Where do any of us come from? We help them to a better future."

"Refugees?" I said addressed to him. "You're smuggling refugees? How many of them arrive alive, huh? After hours, maybe even days inside these things, how many survive, huh? What did you promise them? A better life? If they only gave you their savings, is that it? They gave you all they had, thinking you'd help them get into the promised land? And then what? They'll get arrested and sent back? Or end up in the streets? If they make it that far."

He shrugged. "They know the risks."

I stared at him, startled, appalled. These were

human lives he was talking about. How could anyone be this cruel and still call themselves human?

"Was Wolfe in charge of it all and then handed it down to you?" I paused. "No, wait…he didn't know about the refugees, did he? You added that part later when he retired from the force. He was the one who had made a little extra through selling these appliances and making sure the port authorities looked the other way. He had made a small business out of it, then handed it down to you when he left and couldn't take care of it anymore. But you changed it, and he didn't like it. That's why he had to go. He wanted you to stop what you were doing; it had gotten out of hand. Maybe he even threatened to expose you, am I right?"

"You expect me to answer that?"

"You don't have to. I know when I'm right. So, you had David kill him, but there were witnesses, and you then had to remove them too. But you hadn't counted on Emilia's heart causing Josie to dream about you and how you killed her, and about where to find the body."

"That was an unfortunate turn of events," Ferdinand said. "Everything else was going so smoothly and had for years."

One of his goons made a move, and I grabbed David again, then pulled him close to me, placing the gun against his temple.

Ferdinand signaled for his goon to stand back. "It's too bad, Hunter. You could have been in on it. I would have cut you a deal. We could use someone like you on our side."

"Who else is in on it?" I asked. "Who do you work for?"

That made Ferdinand laugh. "You don't seriously expect me to answer that, do you?"

I pressed the gun against David's temple, hard.

"WHO?"

He laughed again. The sound of his laughter felt like knives to my skin. I couldn't stand the sight of the man. He made me sick.

Still grinning, Ferdinand reached inside his jacket, pulled out a gun, and shot David three times in the chest. David's body went into spasms, and he slid out of my hands. I stood behind, blood smeared on my clothes, then looked up at Ferdinand, eyes wide with shock.

"He ratted me out," Ferdinand said. "He was supposed to kill the girl. That's why he came to your house. But instead, he warned you. Probably because he wanted you to take me down, so he could have everything to himself. I've been expecting him to make his move for a little while now. Now, he can't. And neither can you."

With that, Ferdinand lifted his gun again, pointed it at me, and fired.

Chapter 48

I THREW my body to the ground. The bullet whistled past me, grazing my shoulder as I fell. I landed on my side with a loud thud, panting for air as a regular gunfight broke out.

Once the goons saw that I was still alive, they all simultaneously pulled their guns and shot at me. Luckily, I managed to jump behind a dryer. I heard the bullets hit it on the other side and ricochet off it, causing the bullets to fly everywhere while I crouched down, covering my head.

Once the shooting stopped, I peeked out. That was when I realized the goons hadn't been the ones doing all the shooting, and now most of them were on the ground, some in a pool of their own blood, others screaming in pain, while some were on their knees, holding their hands above their heads, pleading for their lives.

Behind them all stood someone I knew very well. He smiled from ear to ear as he saw me.

It was Fowler.

"Hunter!"

Seeing him, I dared to get out from behind my cover. I walked to him while the officers he had brought moved in and arrested the ones that were still alive. Fowler pulled me into a hug. It felt awkward since he was never much of a hugger; yet it was by far one of the best I had ever gotten.

"Al told me where to find you," he said. "She was worried and had you tracked down, then called me with your exact location. She said you might require assistance. Boy, was she spot-on. We arrived right after you did, SWAT team and everything. We were ready to move in until we heard you two talking. I decided to wait to make sure I heard everything."

"I don't think I have ever been this glad to see you," I said and hugged him back.

"Whoa there, soldier. Don't crush me," he said as I let go of him.

I looked around, then realized something.

"Ferdinand. I don't see him anywhere. Did you book him?"

A SWAT officer came up to us. Fowler asked him, and he shook his head. "Haven't seen him, sir."

My eyes grew wide, and I frantically looked around us. "Could he have gotten away?"

We ran outside, then around the building. There was a big empty space in the parking lot.

"The truck," I said. "There was a big white truck parked here. Where is it now?"

Fowler growled loudly, then turned to his officer. "I thought we had this place surrounded. How did he get out?"

The officer looked confused.

"It doesn't matter now," I said and ran to my car parked behind the next building, then jumped in and roared it to life. I backed out, swung it around, then floored it while calling Al on my phone.

"Al, I need your help."

"Hunter! Where were you? Have you found Josie?"

"I need you to track down a white truck for me using your surveillance cameras. It's leaving the harbor now or left within the past few minutes. Can you do that?"

Chapter 49

"I ALREADY HAVE IT TRACKED DOWN," Al said on the other end.

Putting the siren and lights on, I raced down the road, took a sharp turn, then continued, going down the only road leading out of there.

"What? How?"

"I have it right here on my screen, showing it's driving down MacArthur Causeway, and going onto I95 now, northbound.

"That's great, Al, but how do you know this already?"

"Well, it isn't exactly the truck I'm chasing as much as it is Josie."

"Josie? You know where she is?"

"Yes, she's in the truck, moving up I95."

"What? Why didn't you tell me sooner?"

"Because I didn't know sooner, you fool."

"I don't understand. How do you know now then?"

"Take a right now and get onto I95, continue north," she said.

"Okay," I said and did as she said.

"Listen, I didn't know this till now. I didn't know she was on a truck. I just knew she was at the harbor. When you brought her to my place, I had a feeling I might end up losing her somehow. I told you I'm no good with kids, no matter the age or size. I knew I couldn't keep an eye on her constantly. So, I put a transmitter in her pocket while she slept, one so small she can't feel it, and no one can see it."

"So, you knew she was at the harbor when I left your place?"

"I knew I could track her, and I tried to tell you, but you rushed out of there so fast I didn't get to. Now, if you would have picked up your phone for once in your life, I would have been able to tell you this sooner, but you didn't, and so I called Fowler. He was my last resort since I can't stand the guy, but I had to make sure you were safe."

"So, you're my guardian angel," I said, smiling at the phone, eyes focused and determined on the road ahead.

"Take the exit now," she said. "Get off I95. I found a shortcut. The truck is about a mile ahead of you now, but there's a small traffic jam. You're gaining on him, fast. But you need to get around the jam."

I took the exit, roared across an intersection while cars cleared the way for me, as I came blasting through with sirens blaring and drove back onto I95. I had barely made it when I spotted something in the distance, something sticking up between the cars.

A truck. A big white truck.

"I see it," I said. "I've got him!"

I floored the accelerator once again and came closer still, forcing cars in my way to move to the side. Now, there were only two cars between us. Snorting in anger, I pressed the car to perform to its utmost, and soon I was right behind it, then I pressed up on the side of the truck.

"Come on; come on," I said to the old car as I nudged it along, praying it would soon surpass him.

"You're almost there, Hunter," Al said on the other end. "Now, give it all you have."

But Ferdinand had seen the lights and heard the sirens by now, and he sped up, pressing the truck to go faster. Still, I made it up on his side and could now look directly at him next to me.

"That's right, you bastard," I mumbled while looking straight at him. "I'm coming for you!"

Chapter 50

I SIGNALED for him to stop, to pull over, but he refused. No surprise there. I could hear a chopper approaching in the distance and prayed that it was Fowler, sending assistance.

"STOP, you idiot!" I yelled at Ferdinand, waving my arm wildly. "Before you get us all killed!"

And worst of all, my beautiful daughter.

We approached a car that was driving slower than us, and I had to slow down significantly so that I wouldn't ram into it. Growling, I watched as Ferdinand took off on the inside lane, while I had to wait a few seconds for the car in front of me to shift lanes and let me pass. I groaned and yelled something I knew I wouldn't be proud of afterward, then floored the accelerator. I heard a sound from above and looked up, then realized it wasn't a police chopper, but a news helicopter.

"Where the heck is my backup?" I yelled into the radio. "I need all roads closed on I95 northbound, and air support!"

Dispatch confirmed they were on their way, and as we passed an entrance to the highway, I spotted two police cruisers racing out behind us, just as I drove past them. I reached the back of the truck and sped up to get back up on his side. Seconds later, I succeeded and could once again see his sweaty face inside the cabin, grinning back at me, his eyes manic and crazy.

As I pressed the Chevrolet to its utmost, I finally caught up with him. I pulled the wheel forcefully to the side and rammed into his front left side, knowing very well he was the biggest, and I would probably be the one ending up getting hurt. I just knew I had to try and stop him before Josie was hurt. If he had trapped her in one of those appliances in the back, chances were that she was running out of air, or at least exposing herself to an amount of stress her heart couldn't take at this point. I feared another heart failure, one that would prove to be fatal this time.

The truck swerved to the side but returned to the road just as quickly, this time knocking me forward. My car skidded sideways, turned to the side, and as I looked out the side window, I saw the truck roaring toward me.

I closed my eyes as Ferdinand blasted toward me, then turned the wheel fast and got the car back into its own lane just as the truck roared past me.

Sweat springing from every pore in my face, I stepped on the accelerator once again and drove up on the side of the truck again, trying to repeat what I did earlier. Ferdinand looked down at me, still grinning, then pulled the wheel and knocked into me instead. My car bumped sideways and hit the guardrail. The noise of the car scratching along it hurt my ears, and I let out a loud scream as I tried to regain control of my car. Meanwhile, Ferdinand had been so busy watching me, he hadn't noticed the cars in front of him, and soon he knocked into one of them. There was a terrible noise as he tried to brake, and the truck skidded sideways and crashed into a couple of other cars in front of it before it ran off the road and into the grass.

I held my breath as it roared toward a line of trees, knocking a few of the lighter ones over, cracking them like sticks before it finally met its match in an old magnolia tree and banged into it. The truck came to a sudden halt with a loud crash, and everything stopped inside of me.

Chapter 51

"JOSIE!"

I pushed the door but couldn't open it. I then leaned over and grabbed my Swiss Army Knife from the glove compartment before I crawled to the passenger seat, opened the door, and jumped out into the road. I ran for dear life toward the truck on the side of the road, barely able to breathe because of the fear rushing through me. I knew Josie was onboard that truck somewhere since Al had told me. My only guess was that she was in the back somewhere.

Smoke was emerging from the front of the curled-up truck, but my focus was on the back. The cargo had fallen to the side when it hit the tree. I ran to it, unlocked the hatch, then pulled the doors open and jumped inside.

"Josie?"

The appliances had been tossed around in there like were they nothing but light Lego blocks in a box. A big fridge was right by the door, and the first thing I did was to grab the cardboard box wrapping and cut it open with my knife, then pull it off with everything I had, but it still felt like it was too slow, way too slow. It took forever before I could finally pull it off and open the door to the brand-new fridge.

A set of eyes stared back at me. Someone was in there all right, but it wasn't my Josie.

Leaving the door open so the young woman could crawl out, I exhaled, then climbed over the fridge and moved further inside the truck. I cut open a washer, a dryer, and more people crawled out, some—especially the children—I had to help out. One little girl couldn't even stand on her own two feet; she was so weak. I had to carry her outside, where I hoped and prayed one of her parents were among those that I had set free. Seeing the girl, a woman made a squeal and grabbed her in her arms, and I breathed a sigh of relief.

I then returned inside and found the last box that hadn't been opened. I cut open the wrapping around it, then the box it came in. Thinking there was no way my tall girl would ever fit inside of that small washer, I prepared myself for not finding her. Frantically, I removed the Styrofoam, throwing it everywhere while crying heavily.

Where are you, my sweet Josie? Where are you?

I pulled open the washer forcefully, then peeked inside. The sight that met me was at once sweet and more frightening than anything.

There she was. My wonderful daughter was curled up into a tiny ball inside the washer.

"Josie?" I said, crying. "Josie?"

She wasn't moving. She wasn't opening her eyes.

I reached inside to touch her, then tried to pull her out. Her lifeless body was heavy and hard to move, but finally, I managed to pull her out completely.

That was when I realized she wasn't breathing.

I shook her.

"Josie? Josie? JOSIE?"

I felt for a pulse but found none. Her heart wasn't beating.

I placed her on the floor, then performed CPR, frantically fighting to get her heart back to life again, while calling for help over the radio. Sirens were blaring outside, and more than one chopper was hovering above us.

Josie felt so fragile, so small under my hands; I feared I'd crush her. Yet, I continued, forcefully trying to pump her heart back to life.

"Don't leave me, Josie; please, don't leave me!"

Chapter 52

"DAD?"

It happened so suddenly that I had no idea when or how. I just knew it had happened. At some point, her heart had started beating again, and she was now looking at me with those gorgeous brown eyes of hers.

Never had there been a prettier sight.

I pulled her into a deep hug and held her so tight she started to complain that I was crushing her. I cried and kissed her cheeks over and over again.

"Are you okay?" I asked, looking into her eyes.

"I…I think so."

"Are you sure? You have to be honest with me here, Josie. Does anything hurt? Shortness of breath? Anything?"

She shook her head. "I think I'm fine, Dad."

"You're still going to the hospital. I'm not taking any chances."

"What happened?" she asked, confused.

That was when I remembered Ferdinand. My eyes grew serious as I realized my business here wasn't done.

"Stay here for a sec. Can you do that for me?"

"Where are you going, Dad? Dad?"

I grabbed my gun, then hurried outside. All traffic had been stopped on the highway. Not a car was moving. Firetrucks were parked in the road, and their blinking lights were lighting up the sky, while they were fighting to get someone out of one of the crashed cars.

Police officers were busy attending to the refugees, trying to make sense of the mess. Several of them were leaving in ambulances. I hurried to the front of the truck, then looked inside, wanting to make sure he had either died or that they had gotten him.

The cabin was empty.

I looked around, feeling anxious and worried he might have gotten away in the confusion. I hurried to an officer who was attending to a refugee.

"The driver of the truck," I asked. "Did you book him?"

The officer shook his head. "Not that I know of."

"Did someone else?"

I looked around me, then noticed something on the side of the truck, a handprint of blood like someone had leaned against it.

Someone with blood on their hands.

I hurried back to the cabin, then noticed a trace of blood in the grass that led between the trees.

"Oh, no, you don't," I said, as lifted the gun and followed the tracks.

I ran through the trees, my eyes scanning the area thoroughly for any sign of Ferdinand. He couldn't have gone far, I concluded. He was hurt, and there really weren't that many places to go.

I took a few more steps when something came at me from behind a tree. A metal plate of some sort that Ferdinand could have taken from the crash site slammed right into my face. I felt the pain, and everything disappeared for a few seconds while I tumbled backward before my sight returned, and I saw him standing right in front of me, blood dripping from his arm.

I had barely gotten my focus back when he leaped at me.

Chapter 53

PUNCHES RAINED DOWN ON ME. They were hitting my jaw, my nose, my cheek, shooting pain through me. I managed to get one of my own in, then reach up and grab his chin and push him backward, away from me. I had dropped my gun when he hit me with the metal plate, and I could see it on the dirty ground, but it was too far away for me to reach.

Ferdinand jumped me again and punched me hard on the cheek. My head swirled to the side, and I heard a crack in my neck, but the blow didn't knock me out, and soon I was the one placing one on his nose. The sound of it cracking underneath my knuckles made me wince before I planted a second blow straight to his chin with such great force that he flew backward and slid across the dirt.

This time, he didn't get up again.

I rose to my feet and approached him, looking down at him. His eyes were closed, his mouth open, blood gushing from a wound on his lip. I walked to my gun and picked it up, then turned just as he woke.

I walked back and placed the gun on his head, my nostrils flaring, spitting out blood on the ground.

"It's time for some answers, Ferdinand. I don't believe for one minute you and David were alone in this. Who else is in on it? Who do you work for?"

He mumbled something, then spat out more blood.

"What was that?" I asked.

"I said, you really expect me to tell you?"

I pressed the gun closer to the skin on his forehead. "Yes."

That made him laugh, but I could tell it hurt to do so. "You want me to snitch, huh, Detective? You think I'm gonna answer your questions, let myself be interrogated, cut a deal, do what's best for me, huh? Is that it?"

"Yes. That's exactly what I expect you to do. You know how these things work better than most people."

He exhaled. "I do, Detective. I know how things work, all right. Especially around here."

"So, tell me now, and I might let you live. You know I could just tell them you were trying to escape, which is actually the truth. At least close enough for me to get away with it."

He looked up at me again, grunting and annoyed, then grinned. "Why don't you ask your wife?"

"Excuse me?"

"I said…why...don't...you...ask...your...wife?"

I shook my head, unsure if I had heard him right. What kind of a sick game was this?

"What are you talking about?"

He grinned, showing off his bloody teeth. He had knocked out two of the top front ones, probably from the impact when driving the truck into the tree, and strings of blood were dangling from them.

"You heard me."

"You're lying," I said.

"Really? Think about it. How much do you really know about her?"

I stared down at the pathetic man. I wanted to hurt him so badly, to slap him across the face, but I didn't. Instead, I stared at him, my hand with the gun shaking with anger.

"You don't know anything about my wife," I said. "Absolutely nothing!"

"Probably not then," he said, still grinning. "My mistake."

Faster than I realized what he was up to, he then reached up, grabbed my hands, pressed down on my finger on the trigger, and fired the gun.

Chapter 54

THEY KEPT Josie at the hospital for twenty-four hours to monitor her heart, then sent her home, telling me that everything was as it should be. The heart was functioning as it should, and as long as she stayed away from stressful situations for a few weeks, she'd be fine.

Needless to say, I was very relieved to hear that.

I brought her home and put her to bed so she could take a nap. I sat on the edge, then folded my hands.

"Dear God, thank you for protecting Josie. Thank you for letting me have more time with her here. I wouldn't know what to do without her."

I felt Josie's hand on my arm and opened my eyes. "God knows. He knows you need me."

That brought tears to my eyes, and I kissed her cheek, then sat with her till she dozed off. I liked just looking at her. Jean was downstairs, preparing dinner, and as I walked out into the hallway, I could hear her rummaging around down there. It was a sweet sound. I had told her she didn't need to cook for us, but she had insisted. We had enough on our plate today, she said.

I didn't protest.

I walked downstairs and entered Camille's room. Her eyes lingered on me as I walked in, and I stood for a little while, simply staring at her. She was sitting in her wheelchair; her head leaned against the backrest. She moved her mouth to speak, but nothing but grunts came out.

I had gone through all her stuff upstairs in our bedroom the night before, not sleeping even a little bit. I took every box that belonged to her and went through it, trying to make sense of things. But it had gotten me nowhere. The worst part was that I had no idea if what Ferdinand had told me just before he shot himself had any truth to it…if Camille really knew anything, or if it was just his way of making sure to ruin my life on his way out. If so, he had succeeded. He had gotten to me; that was sure. So many questions piled up in my mind, and I had no way of finding answers.

Yet, I still had to try.

"Why?" I asked her like she understood and knew what I was talking about. "Ferdinand said you knew about those refugees being smuggled in the appliances. Why did he say that? What did he mean?"

Camille stared up at me. Her mouth was open, and

a little drool ran from her lip. I felt so helpless. I had loved her; I had cared for her. We had a child together. She had been the woman for me. And now this? Now, I had no idea what to believe anymore. I hated the way I was looking at her now. I was terrified of the knowledge I had received. Would it make me resent her? Would it make me push her away? And even if Ferdinand was right, could I still judge her for her previous actions? Could it have been something from her past he referred to? Back when she was a drug addict? So much had happened since then. She had changed. At least, I thought she had until she overdosed. But then she had suffered a brain injury; could that have changed her? Or did she belong in jail for what she knew or had done?

And most importantly, could I still love her?

The door opened behind me, and Jean entered. Camille turned her eyes to look at her.

"I'm sorry," she said. "Are you guys talking? Am I interrupting something? I just wanted to take Camille out of her room. I thought she could sit in the kitchen with me. I know she likes to do that from time to time. And it gets her out of this room."

I nodded and wiped away a tear.

"That's very nice of you."

Camille made a loud squealing noise as she usually did when she wanted something. Jean turned to look at her.

"Oh, it looks like she wants the sketchbook. I gave her Josie's a few days ago when I was alone with her, and she seemed to enjoy scribbling on it. Nothing I could make anything of, but I think with a little practice, she might be able to write real letters and maybe, in time, tell us what she wants."

Jean reached over and grabbed the sketchbook, then handed it to Camille along with a pen. Camille groaned, then held the pen in her clenched fist and drew something on the paper.

Jean turned to look at me, then smiled compassionately. "Are you okay? You don't look okay."

"I'm just…pondering about things; that's all."

"Is it the case? About the refugees? Did they not catch everyone involved?" she asked.

I swallowed, then shook my head.

"We're not sure. Some might have been in on it that we don't know about. Those types of things usually spin a lot deeper than what you'd think."

She nodded. "A lot of those they arrested out at the warehouse were officers, right? That's what they said on TV. Some were hired help, but a bunch of them were cops. Bad seeds."

"Yeah, apparently it's been going on for quite some time and reaches deep within the force. It's a mess. I'm not exactly popular in the halls these days for taking down a bunch of my colleagues."

"And Fowler?"

"What about him?"

"You think he was in on it too?"

"No, why?"

She shrugged. "I don't know. It's just that…well, the former major was. Maybe he took over the torch if you know what I mean. They were close, weren't they?"

"I don't think that's the case…" I said. "I've known Fowler for years. I don't think he'd ever…"

"Okay, so let me ask you this. Did you ever find out how they knew where to find Josie when you were hiding her with Al? Did anyone else know where she was? Did you tell anyone else besides Fowler?"

"No, but…he could have told someone; maybe he told Ferdinand?"

She gave me one of those looks. "You really believe that?"

"I don't know, maybe because…"

"And how did Ferdinand get away from the warehouse at the port?" she continued. "The SWAT team had the area surrounded, yet he got to the truck and drove away? Are you telling me someone isn't helping him? I think you have a mole, someone on the inside helping him. Someone high in the ranks. That's what I think."

I exhaled, annoyed. "You watch too many movies."

I said the words in order to stop this conversation, hoping to sweep it off the table. I didn't want to talk to her about this anymore. I wanted this to be over and all the bad seeds found.

Yet, I couldn't help wondering if she was right. She made a strong point. Not one that I liked much. But something wasn't right about this story, and I needed to get to the bottom of it, even though it wasn't going to be easy.

"Anyway, do with it what you want," Jean said, then walked to Camille. "I told you what I think…say, what's that?"

She grabbed Camille's sketchbook, then studied it.

"I think you should see this," she said, showing it to me.

I approached them, looking at the scribbles on the paper. To me, it didn't look like anything, at least not at first. But as I got closer, I could make out what looked like two single words.

KILL ME

I looked up at Camille, then back at the words.

"Kill Me?"

Jean nodded, a sad look in her eyes.

"You want me to kill you?" I asked Camille. "Are you crazy? That's not gonna happen."

Camille groaned loudly, her hand with the pen in great spasms. She was getting agitated, and when she was like that, it was even harder for her to control her movements.

"She's upset. I don't think that's what she is trying to say," Jean said. "Could it be something else?"

"Like what?" I asked, confused. "I don't see what else it could be? She wants to kill me?"

"No, you dummy," Jean said. "I think it means someone tried to kill *her*. Someone tried to kill Camille. It wasn't an accident. She wasn't doing drugs. She didn't overdose."

Hearing this, Camille suddenly yelled, almost screamed at the top of her lungs: "JOSIE! JOSIE!"

I stared at her, puzzled. Jean snapped her finger.

"She keeps saying that, yelling it out. Maybe that's what it means? That's what she's been trying to tell us all this time when yelling out Josie's name? What if she was really trying to tell us that someone tried to murder her?"

My eyes locked with Jean's, and I felt more mystified than ever. Was she right? Had someone tried to kill my wife? Did it have anything to do with what Ferdinand had said? With what Camille knew and maybe had been a part of?

As more and more questions piled up, I felt more confused than ever, especially about who to trust in this town. But one thing was certain. One thing Ferdinand had been right about.

I didn't know my wife at all.

. . .

THE END

Want to know what happens next?
Get ***NO OTHER WAY,*** Book 3 in **the Harry Hunter Mystery Series** here:

https://readerlinks.com/l/1004330

Afterword

Dear Reader,

Thank you for purchasing ***RUN GIRL RUN*** (Harry Hunter#2). This is the second book in a planned series of shorter, more fast-paced mysteries that I'm planning to write. I hope you enjoyed reading it. I know I left you with unanswered questions, but don't worry. Answers will come in the upcoming books as we find out what really happened to Camille.

I know this story is a little extraordinary, and it might be hard to believe, but something like it actually happened. An eight-year-old girl received the heart of a ten-year-old girl who had been murdered. Later, she began having frequent dreams of someone being murdered. The girl was taken to a psychiatrist, and it was later concluded that the girl was talking about a real incident, going into details she couldn't possibly know. After contacting the police, they were able to provide clues like time of death, murder weapon, place, clothes worn by the murderer, and what the little girl had said to him before she died. All that led to the arrest and later conviction of the murderer of the eight-year-old girl.

It's on the verge of being supernatural, but actually, it isn't, according to the scientists and doctors. There are, in fact, scientific reports written about this, and about all the accounts of transplant receivers experiencing a change in nature afterward and dreaming things that their donors lived through. A Dr. Pearsall has collected the accounts of seventy-three heart transplant patients and sixty-seven other organ transplant recipients and published them. You can read more here. This article also goes into possible explanations for the phenomenon. It's very interesting:

https://www.namahjournal.com/doc/Actual/Memory-transference-in-organ-transplant-recipients-vol-19-iss-1.html

You can also read more here:

https://www.iacworld.org/the-scientific-mystery-of-transplant-cellular-memory-projectiological-hypotheses/

Now, the story about refugees being smuggled hidden in appliances is also taken from the real world, believe it or not. Border control between Mexico and the U.S. recently found eleven Chinese migrants inside the furniture and appliances in the back of a truck. It never ceases to amaze me how they keep finding inhumane ways to smuggle people and what refugees will subject themselves to in order to make it. You can read more and see the pictures here:

https://www.cnn.com/2019/12/10/us/california-border-migrants-hiding/index.html

As always, I am so grateful for all your support. Don't forget to post a review of the book if you can.

Take care,

Willow

About the Author

Willow Rose is a multi-million-copy best-selling Author and an Amazon ALL-star Author of more than 80 novels. Her books are sold all over the world.

She writes Mystery, Thriller, Paranormal, Romance, Suspense, Horror, Supernatural thrillers, and Fantasy.

Willow's books are fast-paced, nail-biting page-turners with twists you won't see coming. That's why her fans call her The Queen of Plot Twists.

Several of her books have reached the Kindle top 10 of ALL books in the US, UK, and Canada. She has sold more than three million books all over the world.

Willow lives on Florida's Space Coast with her husband and two daughters. When she is not writing or reading, you will find her surfing and watch the dolphins play in the waves of the Atlantic Ocean.

Tired of too many emails? Text the word: "willowrose" to 31996 to sign up to Willow's VIP Text List to get a text alert with news about New Releases, Giveaways, Bargains and Free books from Willow.

CPSIA information can be obtained
at www.ICGtesting.com
Printed in the USA
LVHW010743260521
688445LV00032BA/1435/J